"Twelve hours ago, a man nearly killed you. He knows where you live. Are you going to trust that he has no reason to come back to finish what he started?"

"If you stay here, we can't... You have to promise—"

"You'll know when I make a promise to you, Annie."

Before she could guess his intent, his hand snaked out to cup the back of her neck. He stroked his thumb against the thumping beat of her pulse.

"I am keeping you safe whether you like it or not. You're right. We are on this task force job together—so you do your brainy thing and I'll do what I do so that you can get us whatever clues you can. I'm tired of this Rose Red bastard and his sick fan club having the upper hand on us. You will not be hurt again. Not while there's breath in my body. Understood?"

USA TODAY Bestselling Author

JULIE MILLER

TACTICAL ADVANTAGE

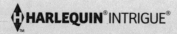

With thanks to my editor, Allison Lyons.
Some books are harder to write than others.
Your patience, insight and support make a difference.
And the Italian food was yummy!

ISBN-13: 978-0-373-74729-0

TACTICAL ADVANTAGE

Recycling programs
for this product may
not exist in your area.

Printed in U.S.A.

ABOUT THE AUTHOR

USA TODAY bestselling author Julie Miller attributes her passion for writing romance to all those books she read growing up. When shyness and asthma kept her from becoming the action-adventure heroine she longed to be, Julie created stories in her head to keep herself entertained. Encouragement from her family to write down the feelings and ideas she couldn't express became a love for the written word. She gets continued support from her fellow members of the Prairieland Romance Writers, where this teacher serves as the resident "grammar goddess." Inspired by the likes of Agatha Christie and Encyclopedia Brown, Julie believes the only thing better than a good mystery is a good romance.

Born and raised in Missouri, this award-winning author now lives in Nebraska with her husband, son and an assortment of spoiled pets. To contact Julie or to learn more about her books, write to P.O. Box 5162, Grand Island, NE 68802-5162 or check out her website and monthly newsletter at www.juliemiller.org.

Books by Julie Miller

HARLEQUIN INTRIGUE

*The Precinct
**The Precinct: Vice Squad
***The Precinct: Brotherhood of the Badge
†The Precinct: SWAT
††The Precinct: Task Force

CAST OF CHARACTERS

Nick Fensom—A KCPD detective with a protective streak that fills every inch of his broad shoulders. He's as baffled by the eccentricities of the brainy Annie Hermann as he is by his attraction to her soulful eyes and curly hair. But what's a man to do when a killer targets the woman he has to work with? He becomes her round-the-clock protector—whether she likes it or not.

Annie Hermann—The quirky criminologist understands science and lab samples better than she understands most people, and has grown used to a lonely existence. When she's attacked while processing the Rose Red Rapist's latest crime scene, it's Nick Fensom who charges to her rescue. But with the two of them sharing a history of getting along like oil and water, can she trust her life—or her heart—to Nick?

Roy Carvello—Annie's neighbor takes his job very seriously.

George Madigan—Nick's uncle is the deputy commissioner of KCPD.

Nell Fensom—Nick's youngest sister.

Jordan Garza—Nell's bad-news boyfriend.

Adam Matuszak—Annie's ex-fiancé didn't think she'd fit in with the life he wanted.

Gobel and Ramirez—What happened to the two cops on duty that night?

Raj Kapoor—A fellow criminologist from the crime lab.

The Rose Red Rapist—His attacks on the women of Kansas City are growing more frequent—and more violent.

The Cleaner—The Rose Red Rapist's accomplice. Psycho fan? Or key to breaking the task force's investigation wide-open?

Prologue

The screech of brakes clawing at the frosty pavement set the driver's teeth on edge as the van up ahead careened around the corner and jerked to a stop near the alleyway by the Fairy Tale Bridal Shop. "Of all the stupid…"

Rolling to a quieter, gentler stop half a block away, the curious driver following the van turned off the headlights and shifted the car into Park. Hugging long arms around the steering wheel, the driver leaned forward to watch the van's door open and see the reckless daredevil climb out. Ethereal snowflakes drifted from the low-hanging sky, turning the illumination from the streetlamps translucent, and making it difficult to pinpoint an exact height for the man, or even determine the color of clothing he wore beyond something dark. But one could make out broad shoulders as he hunched them against the wintry air and looked up and down the street.

The one who watched sank back into the shadows of the car as the man's gaze swept past. His face was obscured by a stocking mask and the puffy clouds of his warm breath in the cold night air. Apparently satisfied that the snow, the holiday and the late hour had chased most of Kansas City's residents inside for the night, he moved to the back of the van and pulled open the double doors.

A rush of adrenaline quickened the hidden watcher's pulse as the mystery man reached inside to pull out a long, cigar-shaped package draped in a blanket or tarp. Catching a breath and holding it, the one who watched without making a peep could see he was clearly up to no good.

He dragged the bulky cargo out of the van and bent his knees to toss it over his shoulder like a duffel bag. After another visual sweep along the sidewalk and street, he carried the rolled-up delivery into the alleyway where he dumped it into a pile of trash bags.

The watcher leaned forward again when he pulled away the covering with all the finesse of a magician revealing his latest illusion. Something tumbled out of the cover and rolled behind the bags, out of sight. Was that…a body?

The watcher gasped.

The pulse was racing now, thundering inside the watcher's ears. Gloved fingers clenched again and again, tighter and tighter, around the steering wheel.

The man wadded up the cover in his arms before unzipping the front of his coat. The spare light from the street barely reached into the alley, so one couldn't be quite sure of the subtle movements, but it seemed he was pulling something out of his coat.

Whatever it might be was small and slender, scarcely discernible in the dim light. He placed the object behind the trash bags, on top of the body. Then he straightened, pulling another object from his coat. He bent forward, backing out of the alley. He held a small windshield brush in his hand and was dusting off the sidewalk, wiping away his footprints and any sign that he had been there at all.

He cleaned up after himself, retreating until he reached the van. The watcher waited for the man to toss the brush and the cover into the back, then quietly shut the doors before hurrying around to climb in behind the wheel and drive away.

A few numbers off the van's license plate were visible through the falling snow. But there was scarcely enough time to write anything down as it turned at the stoplight on the next corner and sped away into the night.

Once the street was quiet again, once the watcher was certain it was safe to move, a cell phone appeared, in case someone needed help. It was clutched tightly in hand as the watcher slowly opened the door. This might not be the smartest thing the watcher had done, but it was by far the bravest.

The winter wind was damp and bitter, biting through wool caps and exposed skin. Big, fluffy flakes of snow clung to the watcher's eyelashes and had to be blinked away. The watcher looked up and down the street, just as the man had done. This particular block was deserted tonight. The interior of every storefront, café and coffee shop was dark. Although, with a tilt of the head, one could see the lights in apartment windows high above, where several end-of-the-year parties or lonely vigils must be happening.

A keening moan rose from the alleyway, snapping the watcher's attention back to the mysterious disposal of trash the curious driver had just witnessed. It *was* a body. Steeling both shoulders and resolve, the watcher hurried across the street.

"Hello?"

A woman staggered out of the alley, clinging to the brick wall for support. Her mouth was bruised and swollen, her lips scrubbed pink. Her hair was a snarled mess, her eyes were glazed. She clasped something sticklike in her fist. "Help me. Please help."

Her words slurred together as if she was high on some drug. When she reached out, the injured woman tripped over her spiky heels and began to fall. But the person who'd followed the van snapped out of shocked immobility and hurried forward to catch her.

"Easy there. Are you all right?" The woman stumbled, knocking the watcher back a step, as well. Hugging arms around the woman to steady her, the would-be rescuer turned her toward the light from the closest streetlamp. There was another cut in the woman's scalp and a puffy red mark beneath one eye. She'd clearly put up a struggle with someone. "I saw that van speeding away. What happened?"

The woman's coat had been buttoned crookedly over her dress. A party dress. Had she been hurt on her way to one of those parties in one of the newly remodeled loft apartments upstairs?

"I've been raped. That man…" Now she could see the slender object clutched in the woman's hand. It was the stem of a blood-red rose. "Oh, my God."

She tossed the flower into the snow and turned away to throw up into the bags of trash from which she'd just crawled.

"Was it the Rose Red Rapist?" the driver from the car asked.

The terror the serial rapist had struck into the minds and spirits of women across the city was evident in the injured woman's wild eyes as she wiped her lips on the sleeve of her coat. "I was on my way to a friend's party…above the florist shop there. They must be so worried. He hit me from behind and…I thought I was being mugged. I've been to one of those women's self-defense courses at KCPD and I…" Tears welled in her eyes, and she pushed her fingers into her hair to brush the scattered tendrils off her face. That's when the driver from the car saw the scrapes on the victim's knuckles from where she'd tried to fight off her attacker. But the wounds had been doctored. In fact, the woman's hands and fingernails had been scrubbed clean. "What did he do to me?" The battered woman saw her sterilized hands and sobbed. "Will you help me?"

"Of course." The driver who'd followed the van wound a supportive arm around the shaken victim to help her walk.

"Are you a cop?"

The watcher guided her back into the alley, farther in than the bags of trash. "Did you see his face?"

The woman's blank eyes suddenly focused. "Yes. I grabbed his mask. That's when he hit me again and I didn't remember anything until I came back here." She grabbed hold of her rescuer and begged. "I need to call 9-1-1. Or there's a bar near here— The Shamrock—but you probably know that."

"Yes. There's a shortcut through here."

"If we turn left…or is it right… Where's my purse? My phone?" She rubbed at the pain that must be throbbing through her temple. The light from the street was fading. The falling snowflakes were barely visible now in the shadows. "It's so hard to think… Wait." She tried to stop and pull away. The watcher from the car let her. The watcher had found what was needed and stooped to pick it up. "What did you say? You're not a cop?"

"I said I'm here to help." The woman's terrified

gaze dropped to the brick in the watcher's hand, understanding coming far too late. "Just not you."

The watcher swung before the woman could scream, and kept swinging until she would never scream again.

Chapter One

"Happy New Year!"

The shouts and whistles and horn blasts from the apartment across the hall drowned out the television program KCPD criminologist Annie Hermann was watching.

As the party from her neighbor's gathering cranked up several more decibels, she twirled her finger in a sarcastic *whoop-dee-do* and watched the lighted ball drop above Times Square. The music leading up to the countdown to the New Year had been entertaining enough, and the pomp and pageantry half a country away had always been a celebration she'd like to see in person one day. But not on her own. And right now, *on her own* seemed like the only option available.

Nothing said "Here's to the promise of a new year" like a twenty-eight-year-old woman sitting at home by herself watching television with her cats while the rest of Kansas City—while the rest of the world—partied together.

She scratched behind the velvety ears of the

Siamese cat nestled in her lap. Her gaze settled on the bare space on the third finger of her left hand. Had it already been two years since the New Year's Eve when Adam had proposed to her? That had been a celebration for the ages. Then she'd spent last year's holiday crying her eyes out because Adam had dumped her. He'd needed to move on, he said—to a new job in a private law firm instead of the public defender's office, to a new life that was more practical and less idealistic than the one they'd envisioned together. He'd claimed he was doing her a favor by leaving her and not forcing her to change into some sort of party-planning, connection-making trophy wife who could be a helpmate for his new ambitions.

Some favor. So what if ending the engagement wasn't her fault? Dumped was dumped.

Feverish tears burned in the corners of her eyes. But she suspected they were more about the sting on her ego than any lingering heartbreak at this point. Or, perhaps, she was indulging in a little pity party because she'd grown far too used to being alone on holidays like this one. And even being part of a mismatch like she and Adam had been was better than a solo celebration of these landmark events.

She stroked the Siamese's warm, seal-brown ears again. At least cats stayed.

"Happy New Year, Reitzie." Blinking away her tears, Annie tucked a curly tendril of chin-length hair that was equally dark behind her own ear and called out through her empty apartment. "Happy New Year to you, too, G.B." But there was no answering meow or rustle of movement. She petted the cat in her lap again and let her gaze wander to all of G.B.'s usual hangouts—the snow boots by the front door, behind the drapes in the second-story bay window, on top of the armoire that housed the TV. "So where is your brother hiding this time?"

Her visual search stopped when her gaze reached the fireplace mantel. Annie smiled. She had no excuse for crying tonight. The framed photograph of a man, a woman and a dark-haired little girl from a Royals baseball game reminded her of happier celebrations from her childhood. Her parents' image smiled back at her. Both of them were gone now, and their time together had been far too short. But it had been the grandest, most loving adventure to be Steve and Amaryllis Hermann's child for eighteen years. "Happy New Year, Mom and Dad."

So maybe she had no family, no fiancé, no date. She had two rescue pets and wonderful memories. She had friends from work and in the neighborhood. Heck, she'd had an invitation to Roy Carvello's party across the hall if she'd really been interested. It wasn't as though she was truly alone.

That was the lie she told herself every time this feeling of isolation from the rest of the world pricked at her spirit.

The rapid gunfire of illegal firecrackers explod-

ing in the courtyard area below her window startled the cat sitting in her lap, spilling both the bowl
of popcorn and the glass of wine she'd just poured
before she could catch either one.

"Reitzie! Oh, man."

A flurry of shouts and applause followed quickly
after as Annie jumped to her feet to right the goblet
and dash to the kitchen to grab a handful of paper
towels. Like she had time to feel sorry for herself.

While the strains of "Auld Lang Syne" filtered
up from the courtyard, a door thumped open across
the hall. Annie dropped to her knees, mopping up
the spilled drink from the hardwood floor and area
rug to the sounds of laughter and mumbled words.
The breathy smacks of sound could mean only that
someone was out there kissing. Then there was a
soft crash against her door that made the pictures
on the mantel rattle before the giggling and laughter and smacking noises retreated.

Correction. Someone was out there making out.

"Party on, dude." Annie lifted her glass in a wry
toast and drank the last swallow of merlot before
pushing to her feet and carrying the goblet and the
wet paper towels to the kitchen sink.

Okay, so maybe she was absolutely and utterly
alone on New Year's Eve. But she took heart in
knowing it was better than being with the wrong
person. She might still be with Adam, fighting to
make something that wasn't meant to be work. He'd
still be trying to fix her and she'd still be com-

ing up short if they'd gone ahead with their marriage plans. So what if she was a little eccentric, a little unsuitable for his well-connected family? Her summa cum laudes and her fellowships had gotten their attention, but ultimately, it wasn't enough. *She* wasn't enough. Her lack of a pedigreed reputation and her desire to work for the crime lab instead of a revered research facility had trumped love. Adam Matuszak had left her.

Just like every other boyfriend of any duration had left her. Just as her parents had left. She *was* alone. She was really, truly, freaking, horribly—

The chirping ring of her telephone from the kitchen wall thankfully interrupted the negative spiral of her thoughts. Holidays were always the worst for her. Three-hundred-fifty-some-odd days of the year she coped just fine on her own. But on Independence Day and Thanksgiving and Christmas and New Year's, she longed to be a part of something—a part of someone else's life without feeling like a charity case or an imposition.

She tossed the wadded-up towels in the trash beneath the sink and picked up the portable phone from its wall-mounted cradle and answering machine.

Recognizing the number of the KCPD task force commander she worked for, Annie took a deep breath to clear her thoughts and tamp down on the nervous spark of anticipation that made her stand up as straight and tall as five feet two inches of height allowed. She inhaled a second time before pushing the talk button and answering. "Happy New Year, Detective Montgomery."

"What? Oh, right. Happy New Year." The veteran detective offered the greeting without altering his no-nonsense tone. "Am I catching you in the middle of a big party?"

The amorous couple bumped against her door again. A quick glance across her quiet apartment revealed one cat creeping out from his hiding place to sample the spilled popcorn, and the other staring daggers at her as though *she'd* been the one to light those firecrackers outside. Some party.

"No, sir. I'm…enjoying a quiet evening at home." She shooed G.B. away from the free food and stooped down to toss the kernels back into the bowl. "Did you need something?"

"Yeah, a favor."

Annie checked the big-faced watch on her wrist. At 12:03 a.m. on New Year's Day?

That spark of anticipation fired through her blood again with a sense of purpose this time, chasing away her nerves. Something bad had happened. Something that made her regret her little pity party. The only favors a senior detective would ask of her would involve her science and someone else's tragedy.

Annie left the popcorn where it had fallen and hurried back to her messenger-style purse on the counter to retrieve her case notebook. She flipped open the pink paisley flap and dug through the catch-all of contents, seeking an elusive pen. "What is it, sir?"

"I know most of the crime lab has the holiday off, but I have a crime scene I need processed ASAP—before the weather gets any worse and destroys what little evidence we might find."

Annie's purse was upside down, the contents tumbling across the quartz countertop when the import of what he was asking registered. "There's been another rape?"

Detective Spencer Montgomery led a group of investigators, public-safety specialists, criminal profilers and uniformed officers in a task force dedicated to solving a string of violent abductions and sexual assaults that had been terrorizing the professional women of Kansas City for several months now. Priority one for the team was to identify and apprehend the unknown subject, or unsub.

"Yes," Spencer Montgomery answered. "Party-goers taking a shortcut through the alley over by the Fairy Tale Bridal Shop found her in the snow." The wind created static over the connection, giving her a better picture of how the elements were deteriorating outside. But the detective's grim pronouncement came through loud and clear. "It's our man. The Rose Red Rapist has struck again."

Annie was the CSI from the crime lab assigned to the elite task force. Although she still did work on other cases, the bulk of her time in the lab was now dedicated to this investigation. She grabbed her boots from beneath the coatrack beside the front door and pulled them on over her jeans.

With a renewed sense of urgency that drove away any lingering mope to her attitude, Annie snatched a pen from the pocket of her coat and jotted down the particulars with one hand while she zipped up her boots with the other. "What hospital did they take her to? I've got a spare kit in my car. I can leave right now and process her."

The ominous crackle of wind stilled her frantic multitasking. "We're taking her to the morgue, Annie."

Her phone tumbled from between her jaw and shoulder. She caught it and set it firmly against her ear. "He's a rapist, not a killer. We determined his last victim had been killed by a jealous boyfriend, not our unsub. Are you sure it's the same guy?"

"The rose I'm looking at says yes."

Annie scooted the cats aside and sank down into her chair. She wasn't sure if she was feeling shock or sorrow or frustration that after three different attacks, they were no closer to being able to identify the rapist than they'd been eight months ago. They'd figured out what type of woman he preyed on. They knew the neighborhood where the Rose Red Rapist chose those women. They knew he abducted them from one location and assaulted them in another, and that he sterilized the victims afterward to remove any trace of DNA. But thus far, the man himself had proved untraceable. "It's bad enough that he's hurting those women, but now he's killing them?"

"Looks that way." She heard the slam of a car door and the windy static on the line suddenly cleared. She didn't have to be a scientist to deduce that the detective had gotten inside his vehicle. "I'm calling all the task force members who are still in town for the holidays. Can you come?"

"Of course." Annie was on her feet again, crossing to the kitchen and tossing everything back into her purse. Work was one place where the loneliness didn't get to her—probably because her science demanded facts, not intuition. Plus, most of the cold, hard truths she dealt with required her to be able to turn off her emotions, whether they stemmed from her lack of a personal life or her empathy for the victims she processed. "I'll be right there."

"I'm leaving a couple of uniformed officers here with a tarp," Detective Montgomery went on. "I'm going to follow the body to the morgue to see if I can get a preliminary report from the M.E.'s office."

Annie hooked the flap of her bag shut and carried it to the coatrack beside her door. The giggles and smooches from the couple on the landing had faded to inconsequential white noise. Her focus now was solely on the task at hand. "Have the M.E. check for trace as soon as possible and send it upstairs to my office at the lab. The cold air should preserve anything that's on the victim, but once she gets inside and the snow on her starts to melt, the water could wash away or compromise anything useful."

"Will do. I'll send Nick over to the crime scene with you until I can get back."

"Nick?" The scarf she was wrapping around her neck suddenly strangled like a vise. She hoped her mental groan hadn't been audible. "Nick Fensom?"

Detective Montgomery's partner and fellow task force member, Nick Fensom, was the sour to Annie's sweet, the oil to her water, the four-wheel-drive Jeep in her energy-efficient green car of a world. Nick Fensom got under her skin like no other man since Adam had—and not necessarily in a good way.

He thought he was funny. He teased, he taunted, he spoke his mind the way most people breathed air—without thinking. And even after working with him on the task force for several months now, Annie still had no clue how to tell when the man was being serious and when he was making a joke. Either way, for some reason, it usually felt like the laugh was on her.

She knew his dark brown hair, deep blue eyes and what was probably supposed to be streetwise charm captivated some women. But she didn't see it. He was probably compensating for his relatively short height—maybe five-nine if he was lucky.

Okay, so she had no room to fault him there; he still towered over her petite height.

But Annie felt no empathy. She clung to whatever predictability and balance she could hold on to in her life, or else she'd sink into those lost little funks like the one she'd been in at the stroke of midnight. She didn't understand Nick Fensom. She had to be on guard against the chaos he brought to her world. And that made him more of a distraction than a teammate, even if they did both work for KCPD and the task force.

"Is there a problem, Annie?" Detective Montgomery reminded her that she'd been silent for too long.

"Um, no." Not nearly as snappy a comeback as Nick Fensom would have come up with. She could do better. She would not let the man get to her, especially when he wasn't even here. "I can manage the scene by myself, sir. You don't need to bother anyone else from the task force. I'm sure Detective Fensom is out on a date tonight."

"He won't be," her commander assured her, much to Annie's chagrin. "Holidays mean family for Nick. Besides, I need as many good eyes here as possible. The snow is coming down harder, and my crime scene is disappearing as we speak."

Fine. For the investigation, for Detective Montgomery and the sake of tonight's unfortunate victim, she'd find a way to make spending time with the irritating, muscles-for-brains detective work.

Bracing herself for the battle of wits and wills where she never quite felt like she was winning, Annie plucked the royal blue stocking cap from her coat pocket and pulled it on over her head. "I'm on my way. I'll meet Detective Fensom there."

Annie had hung up the phone and bundled up in everything but her gloves when the couple in the hallway crashed against her door again. Clearly they were drunk and having a marvelous time getting intimately acquainted. But she had a crime scene to get to. She held her breath and turned the knob, praying she wouldn't see anything too intimate.

As soon as she peeked out, music and conversation blasted her from the open apartment across the landing. Annie shook her head and stepped out, locking her door behind her. "What are you doing, Roy?"

Yes, there were some buttons undone, and the blonde woman's long straight hair was definitely mussed. But her neighbor, Roy Carvello, and his girlfriend du jour had already imbibed too much alcohol to have much success with any personal fireworks tonight.

"Annie!" Roy draped one arm around the blonde and pushed himself upright against the wall with the other. "Happy New Year!"

He slurred the words and stumbled forward, bringing the tall blonde with him. Annie braced one foot behind her and caught him by the shoulders, pushing them both back against the wall. "Easy there, big guy. I don't want either of you tumbling down the stairs."

"You're so nice." Roy's stale beer breath curled the hairs in Annie's nose. He clamped a big hand around her arm and hugged the other woman closer. "S'isn't she nice, Bets-shy?"

Extricating herself from the awkward embrace, Annie smiled up at the drunken couple. "I don't want to see you behind the wheel of a car tonight, okay?" She included the taller blonde in the friendly warning. "You either, Betsy."

"Un-uh," the blonde promised, crossing her finger over the swell of a voluptuous breast.

"'Kay. Happy New Year." Repeating himself, Roy leaned down and planted a stale kiss on Annie's mouth.

Startled, Annie pushed him firmly away. "Oh, gee. You've still got some of those left to go around, hmm?"

"Hey," Betsy protested. "I thought those lips were for me."

"They are, baby." When he turned to capture the other woman's pouty mouth in a kiss, Annie used the directional momentum to guide them back across the landing. But her husky neighbor planted his feet in the open doorway, showing an unexpected bit of focus in his bleary eyes when he looked down at her. "Annie's my friend. My good friend." He flipped up the collar of her coat, tending to her as though he cared. "You headin' out to a party? I wondered why you didn't show up at mine."

Possibly because drunk and loud weren't her favorite things? Or maybe because the first Carvello party she'd gone to had ended up with Roy putting the same moves on her that he was putting on Blondie tonight? Only Annie had been too sober and not nearly as interested in exploring the possibilities as Betsy apparently was.

But he'd proven too nice a neighbor—when he wasn't in party mode—for Annie to hurt his feelings. "Yeah, Roy. I've got someone waiting for me." So maybe that someone was a detective she wasn't really looking forward to seeing. But at least she wasn't lying. "Be safe." She nudged them both into Roy's apartment. She even had a smile for Betsy. "You, too. Remember, no driving."

"Not to worry," Roy promised. "We'll be spending the night right here. Together."

"Oooh, Roy," the woman cooed, sliding her fingers into Roy's dusty-brown hair and pulling him into his apartment.

Feeling grossly uncomfortable, unwelcome and unnecessary as the giggles and kissing resumed, Annie shut the door and hurried down the stairs. After looping the pink strap of her bag over her neck and shoulder, she pushed open the outside door and the shock of the wintry night air nearly stole the breath from her lungs. She pulled on her gloves and waved to the neighbors who were now writing their names in the air with sparklers.

Hunching her shoulders against the bracing wind, she set out across the snow-dusted courtyard toward the fenced-in lot across the street where her car was parked.

She was alone and dateless on yet another holiday, babysitting the grown man next door. Now she could look forward to spending the next few hours with her nemesis, Nick Fensom, and a crime scene where a woman had been brutalized and killed, all while freezing her fingers and toes.

Happy New Year, indeed.

"HEY, GUYS—KEEP IT DOWN, okay?" Nick Fensom apologized for the loud piano music and fourth verse of "Auld Lang Syne" coming from the living room where his family was toasting the New Year with sparkling grape juice and prosecco. He moved down the hallway, farther away from the three generations of Fensoms and extended family who had gathered at his parents' home to celebrate. "Yeah, Spencer, I know the address. Hell of a way for that woman's family to ring in the new year."

"Which is exactly why I'm not letting time or the weather get in the way of finding answers. I'm tired of that bastard staying one step ahead of us."

"You're preaching to the choir, Spence." The piano music stopped and the boisterous conversation among his father's parents, his mom and dad, his mother's younger brother and his own five younger brothers and sisters faded into the dining room and kitchen. Nick opened the coat closet off the foyer and pulled down the metal box where he stored his badge and sidearm whenever he visited the house where he'd grown up. "Let me say some goodbyes here and explain the situation, and I'll be there in twenty, thirty minutes, tops."

"Sorry to tear you away." Although their looks and personalities were as different as night and day, Nick and his partner for three years, Spencer Montgomery, had grown as close as Nick was to either of his brothers. "Did your grandmother make her tiramisu cake?"

Nick chuckled at the rare wistful softening in Spencer's voice. "Stop by the house later today and I'll make sure Grandma saves you a piece."

"I'll do that." Just like that, the glimpse of the human being beneath his partner's buttoned-up exterior vanished. "I'll be at the morgue if you find anything useful. In the meantime, I want you and Annie to go over that alley with a fine-tooth comb. If there's anything—or anyone—close by that makes you suspicious, check it out. And call me."

"Does Pee Wee know I'm coming?"

"It's CSI Hermann. Or Annie." Spencer chided Nick's inclination to tease the petite coworker with the wildly curly dark hair and apparent immunity to his charms. "And yes, she knows. So be on your best behavior. I need her to focus all those smarts on the crime scene—not on trading quips with you."

"I'll mind my manners if she does," Nick promised. "I'm on my way."

He snapped his phone shut and unhooked his belt to fasten on his holster and detective's badge. Then he grabbed his insulated black leather jacket and gloves and headed toward the noise from the heart of the house.

Nick paused for a moment in the kitchen archway to watch his mother, grandmother and oldest sister, Natalie, cleaning up second and third helpings of meatballs and soup and homemade bread. His middle sister, Nadine, was dancing in front of the microwave to whatever tune was playing in her earbuds while she waited for a bag of popcorn to pop. His father got a playful smack on the knuckles and a shooing from the room when he sneaked a molasses cookie from the desserts still on the table. His two brothers, Noah and Nate, and Nell, the baby of the Fensom family, were probably back in the dining room, dealing out another hand of penny-ante poker with their grandfather and Uncle George.

Nick's chest expanded in a sigh that revealed a mix of happiness and regret. His hand drifted down to the gun belted at his waist. He hated to leave the bustle and conversation, the good food and fun. But this was why he answered calls like Spencer's in the middle of the night—to protect his city and the people he loved. The sooner he and the task force could put away the Rose Red Rapist, the sooner he'd stop worrying—a little less, at any rate—about his mother and grandmother and sisters being safe on Kansas City's streets.

But his mother, Trudy Fensom, was equally worried about him once he explained Spencer's phone call and the need to get some eyes on the crime scene ASAP. "That poor woman. But…tonight? It's New Year's."

"Mom, I gotta go. The bad guys don't celebrate the holidays the same way we do." He leaned in and kissed her cheek. "Don't worry. I'll be back for breakfast."

"Be careful, Nicky," his grandmother, Connie, warned.

She got a kiss, too. "Always am."

His dad, Clay, wrapped a sheltering arm around both women and hurried the goodbyes along so Nick could get going. "Keep an eye on the roads, son. Temps are dropping and with this snow there could be patches of black ice."

"I'll watch 'em." Nick crossed into the dining room and gently squeezed his hands over the shoulders of the silver-haired grandfather whose name he shared. "I'll be back for a rematch with you, card shark."

"Everything okay?" George Madigan, a cop like Nick, who'd been on the force long enough to recently be promoted to deputy commissioner, pushed back his chair. Even though his uncle had been pushing papers at KCPD headquarters the past few years, the detective instincts were still there. "The department's short-staffed tonight. You need backup?"

Nick urged his uncle back to his seat. "Just some task force business to take care of," he answered, keeping the details vague for his younger siblings while dropping enough of a hint to let George know what he was up to. "I've got it covered."

George's steely gray eyes narrowed with suspicion. "You're sure?"

"Yes, sir. Besides, somebody's gotta keep an eye on this one." He patted his grandfather's shoulder and pointed a warning finger to his brothers and sisters sitting around the table. "You all keep him honest. He's dealing off the bottom of the deck."

Nicolas Fensom snorted at his grandson's ribbing. "I am not. Fifty years of playing poker just makes me good."

And then Nick realized the numbers around the table really didn't add up. "Where's Nell?"

"She got a text from——"

"Damn it, she's seeing that boy——"

"What boy?"

"She's in love, Grandpa."

"She's seventeen."

"If she snuck out again——"

"Easy, Dad." Nick held up his hands to stop his father from charging through the house, and cool the collective concern in the dining room. "I'm sure it's nothing."

"She's missed curfew more than once because of him. Taking calls at all hours—sending my texting bill through the roof. I don't like him."

The same sense of alarm had already energized Nick. For one night, for *family* night, she couldn't give that rebellious streak of hers a rest?

Nadine jogged back down from a quick run upstairs. "She's not in her bedroom. But her coat's still here."

Nick nodded to George to keep his brother-in-law in check and sprinted toward the front door. "I'll find her."

The blast of cold air was just what Nick needed when he stepped out onto the big wraparound porch and saw his baby sister leaning up against the fender of a souped-up Chevy Impala parked in front of the house. A young Latino man with his cap on sideways was leaning up against *her* with their lips locked together.

Ah, hell. Was that a number 7 inked into the back of his neck? He'd worked gangs before being partnered with Spencer and joining the task force. But he didn't need that kind of training to recognize the signs of trouble for his youngest sister.

"Nell?" he shouted, taking the steps two at a time down to the front walk. His sharp voice, his bold stride or maybe the brass badge peeking out from the open front of his jacket, were motivation enough for the young Don Juan to take a step back from his sister.

"Oh, great," she moaned, tucking her long brown hair behind her ears. "The cops are here. Did Dad call 9-1-1?"

"Where's your coat?" Nick asked, ignoring the attitude. He glanced at the fluffy white flakes settling onto Nell's blue sweater, and wished he had enough cause to do a pat-down on the black parka and baggy jeans on Romeo here. He glanced from Nell's petulant blue eyes up to Romeo's dark brown ones. The younger man might top him in height by a good six inches, but the parka and jeans were hanging on a wiry thin frame and Nick knew he could out-muscle the kid if he had to. "Are you going to introduce us, sis?"

"Nicky, we didn't do anything wrong." Her shoulders huffed in protest when she realized he wasn't budging. She pulled the sleeves of her sweater down over her fingertips and hugged them beneath her arms to keep them warm. "This is my oldest brother, Nick."

"I'm Jordan Garza, Officer." Good. So Romeo *had* seen the badge. Instead of shaking hands with Nick, though, he plunged his into the pockets of his coat and grinned. "Every girl deserves a kiss on New Year's Eve. Especially *my* girl."

He winked at Nell. She pursed her lips and blew him an air kiss.

When had Nick's high-school-aged sister become such a flirt?

Opting to slide his gloves onto his chilling fingers instead of hauling her bodily back inside, Nick tamped down on a protective surge of temper. If this had been a routine stop of strangers in the street, he'd be thinking about their safety before his own irritation with the situation. "Get in the house before you freeze, Nell. Everybody's waiting for you."

"I've had enough party games and talking about the old days," she protested, her words stuttering as she began to shiver. "I want to say good-night to Jordan."

Nick waited for the alleged boyfriend to notice the pale cast to Nell's cheeks and the way her jaw trembled with the cold. Chivalry was dead in the 'hood, apparently. Nick shrugged out of his own jacket and draped it around Nell's shoulders. "Why didn't you just invite him to the party instead of sneaking out?"

She shrugged off Nick's coat and linked her arm through Jordan's to snuggle up to him. She rolled her eyes up to the stern father and curious family members silhouetted at the front windows. "Like he'd be welcome here?"

"Have Mom and Dad even met him?" The bite of winter wind pierced the double layers of sweater and long-sleeved tee Nick wore, but he kept his jacket in his hand to warm up his sister the moment she'd let him. If she came to her senses any-time soon. "So, what? You were going to take off with this guy after midnight and go to his place?"

"There aren't so many rules at my pad," Garza bragged.

"Are there any parents? Any guardian in charge?"

"*I'm* the man of the house." Jordan thumped his chest and unzipped his coat. Recognizing the movements that could signal a call for backup from other gang members, Nick dropped his jacket to rest his hand on his Glock and visually sweep the street for any signs of movement. "Easy, Officer." Jordan's hands were heading for the deep pockets of his jeans now. "I ain't got no big brother buttin' into my business."

"Keep your hands where I can see them, Garza." Nick altered his stance to face the potential threat head-on. He wrapped his fingers around Nell's arm and pulled her away from the gangbanger. "I think you'd be smart to go home now."

"Nicky—" She tugged against his grip.

"You threatening me, brother?"

"Hands, Garza." Nick tightened his grip on his sister and pulled her behind him. "Get in your car and drive away."

Jordan pulled his hands from his pockets and held them up in surrender despite his defiant tone. "I'll see her at school."

"Yeah, well, you won't see her here. Not tonight.

It's too late for her to be out. Besides, this is family time."

"*You're* leaving," Nell argued.

"I'm working," Nick clarified.

Her shoulder sagged with a dramatic sigh. "This is so embarrassing."

"It's cool, babe. Relax. They ain't comin' between us." Jordan reached out and Nick jerked Nell beyond his reach.

"Nicky, please."

Relenting for one moment at the soft-voiced plea, Nick let her step forward. His eyes followed every movement as the younger man stroked a finger across Nell's cheek.

"I'll call you tomorrow," Jordan promised.

But Nick drew the line at letting his baby sister run into her boyfriend's arms. "Good night, Garza."

"Later, brother."

Nick pulled his sister back from the curb as Jordan climbed in behind the wheel and revved the engine loud enough to wake any neighbors who might have turned in early. Only when the Impala was a block away and he was sure there were no other allies in cars watching after Garza or the house did Nick release his sister.

Nell wheeled around to face him, shivering with a mix of cold and anger. "That was rude."

"You're talking about him, right?"

"Are you done humiliating me now?"

"The kid's got gang tats, Nell." He scooped up

his jacket off the ground and brushed away the clinging snow. This time she did let him drape it around her shoulders. "And you're dating him?"

"Jordan's gang life was years ago, when he was in middle school. He's not like that anymore."

"He's still dressing and driving the part." He rubbed his hands up and down the sleeves of his sweater, needing to find some warmth for himself.

"You know, you don't live here anymore." The blue eyes that matched his own tilted up with a soft expression that had always wrapped him around her little finger. Her voice softened, too. "You don't even know Jordan."

"And why is that?" He pulled the jacket collar together at her neck and switched the massaging warmth to her shoulders. "I can't give him a chance if you don't bring him around. Is there some reason you don't want him to meet me?"

"Daddy's already freaking out about him. I don't need you breathing down my neck, too." Her crooked smile reminded him of when she'd been a little girl and big brother could do no wrong. "I'm seventeen now. I don't need every moment of my life chaperoned anymore."

"How old is Jordan?"

She let go with a noisy sigh. "Why should I answer? You're just gonna go look him up on your crime-fighting computer when you get to work. That isn't fair."

"Is he eighteen? If he's of age and you two are…"

Oh, man, he couldn't think of his baby sister being with a guy yet. "If you two are serious, then he could be in some legal trouble."

"I never asked his age."

"Please tell me he at least *goes* to your school and doesn't just show up afterward to pick you up."

The attitude was returning. "He's a senior."

"Look, I don't mean to be hard-nosed about this, but he's not making a good first impression."

"How could he? You practically pulled your gun on him."

"He looked like he might have been armed." Nick stepped closer. He could do the attitude thing, too. "In my job, you don't get second chances if you let the bad guy get the drop on you. If he's still tied to a gang, Mom and Dad are right to be concerned about this guy becoming a part of your life. I'm trying to protect you."

She groaned on three different pitches before swinging off his jacket and shoving it into his chest. "I don't know if it's worse for you to be a cop or my big brother." Nell stormed up the stairs onto the porch. "Jordan's a good guy. I love him. But don't worry, I'm not sleeping with him." Thank God for small favors. "Yet."

Nick swore. "Nellie Fensom!"

But she waltzed away into the house—beyond his words, beyond his reach, beyond his understanding. Nick's heavy breath clouded the cold air around him. When it cleared, he exchanged a look with his father. He hated leaving with his sister mad at him and his father looking as helpless as he felt about keeping the headstrong teenager safe. Nick wanted to restore the harmony of the evening they'd all shared earlier.

But he had to leave. Spencer was counting on him to be his eyes and ears at the scene of another rape and murder. He wasn't about to let his partner down. He wasn't about to let the victim's loved ones go without answers.

But he wasn't used to leaving his family when they needed him, either.

Nick pulled on his jacket and zipped it against the cold as he headed for his Jeep. "One problem at a time," he silently promised everyone who needed him tonight. "One problem at a time."

Chapter Two

"What's your problem, Hermann?" Nick Fensom's deep-pitched voice teased her from above. "I've already canvassed apartments on both sides of the street, and you're still in the same spot where I left you."

Annie glanced up from the alley where she was working and glared at the stocky, dark-haired detective casting a shadow over her open evidence kit and work space. The tarp tenting over their heads from one wall of the alley to the other snapped with the wind and strained against the ropes she'd tied off like full sails on a seagoing schooner. She was knee-deep in trash bags, blood spatter and blowing snow—her cold fingers shaking as she struggled to open a paper evidence bag so she could drop the beaded evening purse she'd found beneath the nearby Dumpster inside. She pulled the flashlight she held between her teeth out of her mouth to answer.

"Well, let's see, Detective Smart Mouth. It's cold. It's windy. It's snowing. Can you piece together the

clues and figure out why this is taking so long?"
She could do sarcasm, too. "You got the easy gig,
spending a couple of hours inside where it's warm
and dry."

"And crashing parties or waking up surly, annoyed building supers and frightened tenants."

Annie scoffed at his trials and tribulations. "It's
not my fault if you showing up ruins a party and
scares little old ladies."

He deflected the zinger with a smug grin. "Actually, I was invited to join a couple of New Year's
celebrations. I was also asked to arrest the noisy
neighbors on the floor above one apartment. And
there was a nice Mrs. O'Halloran who invited me
in for champagne and cookies if I was interested.
I had to tell her I was still on the clock and, regret-
tably, turned her down."

Point to Fensom. Annie bristled. Her only invitation tonight had come from the lecherous drunk
neighbor across the hall. "No one's stopping you
from leaving. I bet Mrs. O'Halloran's cookies are
still toasty warm if you want to go sample them."

"She was older than my grandmother, Hermann.
You know, anybody overhearing our conversation
might think you don't like me."

"There's no one listening in, so I don't have to
pretend to make nice."

Point to Hermann. The teasing grin vanished,
and for a split second, Annie was tempted to apologize. But a man with that much self-confidence

couldn't really be offended by the quips they routinely traded each time they were forced to work together, could he? Rather than explore the possibility that there might be a sensitive human being beneath that cocky charm, Annie opted to change the topic.

The idea that she and Nick Fensom truly were alone in the middle of this wintry night in a place where a dead body had lain only hours earlier sent a little shiver of unease down her spine. It merged with the chill that vibrated her grip, and she swung her light toward the yellow crime scene tape at the end of the alley. "Where did the two uniformed guys go?"

"Relax, Hermann, I've got your back for a few minutes." He tilted his head toward the cross street at the end of the block. "The Shamrock Bar is just around the corner. They started serving free coffee and snacks after 1:00 a.m. in case anyone's been partying too hard tonight. I sent the officers to get four coffees and give them some time out of the cold."

She'd like to dive into a bath-sized pot of hot coffee right about now. Including her in the drink run was an unexpected consideration that took the edge off the defensive hackles Nick's presence inevitably raised in her. "I suppose they've been out here longer than either one of us. They've earned the break."

Still, sterile plastic gloves were no match for

hours of working in the wintry night, photograph-
ing potential evidence, digging through bags of
garbage and cataloguing everything she'd found
thus far. The bag she'd been fighting with refused
to open for her stiff fingers. The knees of her jeans
where she kneeled had soaked through to the skin,
and the tendrils of hair sticking out from beneath
her stocking cap had kinked around her face and
stuck to her cheeks with the precipitation in the air.

Meanwhile, other than the puffs of warm breath
that clouded the air around his head, Detective Fensom looked solid and warm and vexingly unaf-
fected by the dropping temperature.

As if reading her condemning thoughts, Nick
turned the banter back to the job. The beam of his
flashlight joined hers to better illuminate her work.
"What do you have there?"

"I found the victim's purse." Giving up on the
paper sack for now, Annie lifted the camera hanging from her neck and snapped a picture of the
beaded evening bag wedged between the rear wheel
of the Dumpster and the alley's brick wall. Then
she picked up the bag and opened it. "Clearly, this
wasn't a robbery." She pulled out three neatly folded
twenties and a credit card. A driver's license, five
business cards, a comb and lipstick rounded out
the contents. Annie read the name on the license
and business cards. "Rachel Dunbar. Twenty-seven
years old. She was an investment analyst."

"A successful professional woman. That fits the

victim profile of the women the Rose Red Rapist targets."

Annie returned the contents to the purse and picked up the evidence bag again. Juggling the purse, the bag and her flashlight with her frozen hands proved to be a challenge, but it didn't stop her mind from speculating. "Why is there no phone here? I wonder if she had a cell phone in her coat or if the killer took it from her. I can't imagine a woman going out at night on her own without a cell."

"When I check in with Spencer, I can ask if the phone was on the body. I'm guessing her attacker took it from her, though," Nick speculated. "It keeps her helpless, at his mercy. Our unsub is all about control and dominance over the women he assaults. He obviously can't have her calling 9-1-1."

Frowning, Annie nodded toward the bag already tucked into her evidence kit. "So he takes the phone, but leaves the brick he killed her with? I always thought our guy was smarter than that. It doesn't make sense."

"Let's gather the evidence first and analyze it later." Nick knelt beside her, the bulk of his shoulders and chest blocking the wind as he plucked the sack from her fingers and opened it for her. Annie's fingers were still shaking as she jotted down the time and date and signed the sealed bag. He dropped the sack inside her kit and reached for her hands. "I need to get you out of the cold, too. How much more do you have to do?"

Annie's mouth opened in surprise as he tucked her flashlight into the CSI vest she wore over her coat, and pulled off his leather gloves to capture her fingers between his palms. "What are you doing?"

He peeled off her latex gloves next. "What does it look like?"

Gasping at his firm, yet light, touch, Annie was stunned into silence. Nick Fensom had never touched her before, other than an accidental brush of contact as they passed each other in a crowded room or handed off a file folder at a meeting. And now he was holding her hands and instilling warmth as if he had some proprietary claim to do so.

The gentle massage of Nick's bigger fingers over hers was almost painful as the blood began to warm her heat-deprived extremities. A little hiss of pain brought his gaze up to hers. "Easy, slugger. You're okay."

"Slugger?" A baseball reference?

He glanced up at the blue-and-white *KC* on the cuff of her stocking cap. "Looks like you're a Royals fan."

"I am."

"Me, too. Who'd have thought you and I had something in common?"

"Yeah." Witty comeback. But her thoughts were

shifting from shock into the critical observations that usually filled her mind.

Sensation returned to her hands and Annie began to feel every supple movement of his fingertips, every callus that marked his broad palm. She could feel the heat radiating from his body, from his skin into hers.

Nick Fensom was being nice? On purpose? Where were the wisecracks that forced her to stay on her mental toes? The annoying arguments that threatened to undermine her investigative expertise? The heat he rubbed into her once-numb hands was blossoming elsewhere inside her, too. Her cheeks began to thaw with the traitorous flush of her physical response.

Up close like this, Annie noticed just how blue Nick's eyes were. Their dark cobalt color was emphasized by the shadows between them, yet there was a sparkle of energy there, a light that gave them a sharp contrast to the coffee-brown darkness of his hair. And maybe it was just the close proximity she wasn't accustomed to—or the thickness of his insulated leather jacket—that distorted the dimensions of his body. She knew he hadn't grown any taller, and yet his shoulders and chest were broader than she remembered. They were wide enough to block the worst of the wind and snow and allow the air between them to warm and fill with the scents of the sterile solutions she used, along with the leather and faint garlicky deliciousness emanating from him.

"You're like a furnace," she noted, drawing her focus back to the reviving heat of his fingers around hers. Was he feeling this unexpected jolt of awareness, too? "Why are you doing this?"

"Speeding the process so I can get out of here before dawn. Your hands are like ice."

"Oh." So she'd been analyzing the color of his eyes and wondering if the dark stubble dusting the angles of his face would be sandpapery or soft to the touch while he'd simply wanted to get out of here sooner. *Awkward.* He probably had a hot date he'd left in a snug apartment somewhere, and Annie's poky thoroughness was keeping him from getting back to her. With plenty of embarrassment to infuse her blood and keep her warm now, Annie jerked her hands from his and grabbed a fresh pair of gloves from her kit. "I'm fine. You can stop."

"I don't mind." She flexed her fingers and reached up to extricate her flashlight from the net pocket in her CSI vest where Nick had stuck it. But her hands were chilling again and he'd jammed it in there good and why the heck couldn't she manage her own equipment? Nick plucked the flashlight from her vest and pressed it into her palm. "Here. We're part of a team, right? We have to help each other out."

"Right." *Go ahead and be practical and coordinated and temptingly warm,* she accused him silently, pushing to her feet and feeling about as graceful and misguided as a teenage girl who'd just had a run-in with her high school crush. She must be suffering from hypothermia to have hallucinated any sort of fascination with Nick Fensom. "I'm almost done. The path of blood droplets I was following has tapered off considerably."

"O...kay." He drawled out the word, clearly questioning her abrupt retreat. Nick pulled on his black leather gloves and straightened beside her. "By the way, you're welcome."

Annie lifted her gaze from the void of snow on the bricks behind the Dumpster. "Sorry." Rubbing her hands truly had been a nice gesture, which was certainly more observant of her discomfort and more considerate than she'd given the burly detective credit for being. "You didn't have to do that, but I appreciate it. I'll do my best to get done *before* daylight, so we can both get someplace warm."

And so she could find some time to herself to remember that Nick was just a cop she worked with, a streetwise pain in the posterior she frequently butted heads with—not the man who had suddenly blipped onto her sexual-awareness radar with his big shoulders and blue eyes and surprising consideration.

"Sounds like a temporary truce to me."

Annie nodded her agreement, savoring the cold slap of wind on her face that brought her thoughts back into focus. She bent closer to the bricks as the bare spot took shape. It was a handprint, dotted with a few weeping trickles of blood. There was another handprint, another smear of red, climbing up the wall to where the falling snow clung to the bricks above the Dumpster and covered up the rest of the pattern. "This has been moved. Our vic got to her feet and pulled herself up along the wall here. And…something else."

Nick waited for Annie's nod before putting his shoulder to the Dumpster and shoving it aside a couple of feet. Then the beam from his flashlight joined hers. "That second handprint's bigger. Looks like a scuffle to me. Two people fell against the wall—caught themselves. But this can't be where she was killed. There isn't enough blood."

"That blood pool is farther back in the alley. She had her head bashed in back by where the alleys cross, beyond any line of sight from the street— with the brick I bagged up in my kit, I'm guessing. These are something different." With her sterile gloves still in place, she tested one crimson spot with her fingertip. "The drops here aren't as tacky. They've been here longer. This may be the initial attack site."

"Where he first abducted her and hauled her away to a secondary location to rape her." Nick's shoulder nudged hers as he came in for a closer look. "Maybe this one got a look at her attacker, and they struggled. Could that be our perp's handprint?"

Nudging him back out of her way, Annie focused

the camera hanging around her neck and snapped a photograph. "I doubt we'll get any fingerprints from our unsub—the lines are blurred enough that I'm sure both were wearing gloves. Wait a minute."

"Did you see something?"

Before Nick could finish his question, Annie grabbed his wrist and pulled his hand in front of the prints on the wall. "Hold that right there."

Before he could voice another question, she'd snapped another picture.

"Now take your glove off and hold it up there."

She didn't miss the dubious arching of his brow, but Nick did as she asked. "And my hand is photogenic because?"

"It's a comparison shot." Next, she photographed her own hand in front of the bloody prints on the wall before stooping down to pull a tape measure from her kit. "The smaller prints are about the size of my hand, so I'm guessing they belong to the victim. We can verify that once I talk with the medical examiner. But the other print is considerably larger."

"Man-size hands." Nick regloved and stepped to the side, clearing out of her work space. "The rapist's?"

"Possibly." She recorded the exact measurements in her notebook and stuffed it back into her coat pocket. "It's something we can compare if we find handprints at other locations, or we bring a suspect into custody."

"That's not much."

Annie refused to be so pessimistic. "It's more than we had a few minutes ago."

"So why bring Rachel Dunbar back here to kill her? He could have done it in the privacy of whatever hellhole he takes his victims to." The beam of Nick's flashlight followed her as Annie pulled a swab and Luminol from her kit to verify that the spatter and smears on the wall were blood. "Leaving the body here feels like he's showing off what he can do. Rubbing it in our faces that KCPD hasn't been able to break the case yet."

Shuddering at the disturbingly blunt commentary, Annie suggested an explanation of her own. "From the account of Bailey Austin, the first victim the task force worked with, she was raped at a building that was either being built or remodeled—where there were signs of construction. She remembered a clear plastic drop cloth that covered everything. He's keeping that location clean—traceless."

So why be less cautious about the evidence here?

"If it's a construction zone, he'd have work crews coming and going who might find the body—or at least recognize that something violent happened there." Nick snapped his nimble fingers as an idea hit him. "Plus, the walls and layout could be changing daily. My dad's a contractor. I've seen empty lots become complete houses in a week. It'd be damn near impossible for a witness to give an accurate description—the whole layout might change before we could follow up on it."

"It has to be someplace that's familiar to him. Or maybe the location is someplace he created specifically for these assaults." Two drops of Luminol turned the cotton swab a telltale purple. Definitely blood.

"You think the rape is part of some kind of ritual?" Nick's gaze narrowed. "That there's a special significance to where the Rose Red Rapist takes his victims?" He turned the beam of light into the depths of the alley, swinging the flashlight from one strip of yellow crime scene tape to the strip blocking the front sidewalk. "So what's all this then, Sherlock? A bloody coincidence? Our guy hasn't made mistakes or left this much evidence behind before."

Sherlock? Annie glanced up. Nick's dark hair and the charcoal-gray heather scarf he wore were getting dusted with the snow coming in at the edge of the tarp. She prided herself on noticing the details of her surroundings, but those keen senses were supposed to be focusing on a murder scene, not the detective demanding answers from her. The frigid temps must really be addling her brain. She forced herself to look away and point out the bags labeled and stowed in her kit. "I don't know. This is different from the other crimes scenes I've investigated. I've never had this much trace before. It's almost as if…"

"As if what?"

Annie shook her head. "I don't like to speculate."

"Humor me."

"It's as if we've got two crime scenes in one location. The abduction, which could account for the handprints on the wall here, and the murder..." She turned her own light toward the darkness at the back of the alley, where a second tarp did what it could to protect the evidence there. "Which happened back there."

"And all the blood is the vic's?"

"I don't know yet. There's an awful lot. I'd have to—"

"—analyze it." Nick muttered the end of the sentence as though he was impatient to move on to a new topic. He brushed the snowflakes off the top of his hair, leaving shiny dark spikes in their wake. To her surprise, he seemed to give her idea some merit. "Dr. Kilpatrick believes there's more than one unsub we should be looking for."

Annie recalled the conclusion reached by the forensic psychologist assigned to the task force when she'd been investigating the Rose Red Rapist's last attack before tonight's grim events. "She thinks there are two different profiles to these attacks, indicating more than one man is involved in the crimes—the rapist and someone who cleans up after him. This could be trace from the initial abduction. And if Rachel Dunbar struggled—meaning he didn't knock her out with one blow the way he usually subdues his victims—then it could have been a messy confrontation, giving the cleaner more impetus to silence the one woman who could possibly identify the rapist."

"The Cleaner?" Nick's blue eyes glowed with something that looked like derision. "You've given our accomplice a nickname? Better not let the press get wind of that." He thumbed over his shoulder toward the dark storefront across the street. "They've already given our perp a cutesy name because the first rape happened outside the Fairy Tale Bridal Shop."

Annie pulled up to every centimeter of her five feet two inches of height. She hadn't been trying to glorify the perp's cleverness or give the press any more fodder for sensational headlines. She had simply been stating facts. "Like I said. It's just speculation. I'm trying to figure out what the evidence says."

"And it's telling you we have two crime scenes at one location." Maybe that skeptical gleam was Nick's deep-thought expression because it sounded like he was actually agreeing with her theory. "One from the Rose Red Rapist and one from an accomplice in some freaky sort of tag team. Could be a crazy fan who wants a taste of that violence, too."

Annie stooped down to replace the Luminol bottle in her kit and take out unopened swabs in sterile cases to obtain fresh samples of the blood smears for typing and DNA analysis. "It sounds kind of sick, but it looks to me like we've got a rape addict and some sort of enabler."

"Now there's a dysfunctional relationship." Nick swore. "I liked it better when we were after just one nutcase."

"It's only a theory," Annie hastened to clarify, dabbing at the bricks. "I can't prove the identity of the second attacker or what his motives might be yet. I can't even confirm that there *was* a second man in this alley tonight."

"But your gut tells you Dr. Kilpatrick is right— that there are two attackers?"

Annie snapped the vials shut and pulled the marker from her pocket to label them. She slipped them all into her pocket, exhaling a sigh that clouded the air between them. "The evidence seems to indicate that."

Nick nodded, apparently satisfied with her assessment of the crime scene. "Finish up here. I'm going to call Spencer and see if he convinced an M.E. to come in early and look at the body yet. I'll ask for a quick measurement of the victim's hand size so we can speed the identification of those prints." He pulled his cell phone off his belt, giving her a glimpse of the weapon holstered beneath his jacket. "When the uniformed officers get back, I've got some more doors to knock on. Will you be okay if I leave you here for a few minutes to make a couple of calls?"

Being left to fend for herself felt all too familiar. She'd had a lot of practice over the years putting on an equally familiar brave smile. "I'm okay on my own."

But he was already backing toward the sidewalk at the front end of the alley. "I won't go too far. Holler if you need me."

"Don't scare anybody while you're out there." The teasing remark felt much more normal than the memory of friendly conversation and his warm touch still moving through her veins.

"Don't freeze your nuggets." He gave it right back with a wink and a grin, flipping open his cell phone as he disappeared around the corner. "Yo. Hey, can you connect me to…"

More certain of her actions as a criminologist than of her *re*actions to Detective Fensom, Annie stepped back to snap another picture of the blood spatter and snowy handprints on the brick wall.

The camera's mechanical noises and the pop and snap of the blowing tarps covered the soft staccato of something shuffling around in the back of the alley where it bisected another throughway between buildings. Somewhere in the darkness beyond the T-shaped intersection, a lid got knocked off a trash can and hit the snow-packed pavement. Startled by the noise, her pulse picked up speed as the metal disk spun around and around until it stilled into silence. Only then did she release the breath she'd been holding.

"Wind must have caught it," she hypothesized on a whisper.

Annie lowered her camera and peered into the black hole at the end of the alley. Several seconds of answering stillness tempered her initial alarm and she relaxed and returned to her work. Backing up, she adjusted her camera to take a wide shot of the handprints on the brick wall. A soft whirring sound brought the image into focus. A click snapped the picture.

Muffled footsteps, crunching over the snow, scurried across the back of the alley. Tensing at the new disturbance, Annie swung her gaze around into the darkness. "Hello?" She wracked her brain to come up with the names of the two officers she'd met earlier, blocking off the alley. "Officer Galbreath?" She couldn't come up with the second name. "I hope you brought coffee."

No answer.

No sound besides the wind and tarp, either. She should have been able to breathe easier. But that wary uneasiness wouldn't leave her.

Because she'd had no luck spotting the unwanted company with her flashlight, Annie raised her camera and snapped a photograph. She glanced down at the small digital screen. Shadowy blobs darker than the middle of the picture lined either side of the alley. Trash cans and power poles most likely.

Probably nothing to worry about.

But there was something else, farther back, its

shape distorted by the ruffling tarp, framed in the tee where the two alleys connected. The hair at her nape pricked to attention. She raised her gaze from the camera to the tunnel of shadows leading down to the dim light at the crossroads.

Someone was moving in the other alley.

"Officer Galbreath?" The second name popped into her head. "Foster?"

It made sense for the two officers to take a short-cut coming back from the Shamrock Bar, as cold as it was. No one else would cross the yellow crime scene tape blocking each end of the alley, would they?

No one she wanted to run into, at any rate.

Screw independence.

"Detective Fensom?" She retreated a step toward the sidewalk and called over her shoulder. She wondered if he was still on his phone to his partner. Had he been a rat and gotten inside his Jeep to warm up while he made the call? "Nick?"

Speaking of rats, maybe that's all this was. Even though she didn't particularly want to meet a swarm of those either, it would be a plausible explanation for the sounds—rats tunneling beneath trash bags, rifling through Dumpsters and knocking things over.

She almost hoped that she'd step on a rat or some other critter to prove to herself that any threat she felt was only in her imagination. But a rat would still be moving. And the only thing she was hearing now was her own pulse throbbing in her ears.

"Nick?" A shadow darted around the corner and rushed toward her. Way too big to be a rat. "Nick!"

Annie was in full retreat as the figure dressed in black charged. She raised her flashlight, the only weapon she had on hand as the black coat and dark eyes behind a stocking mask took shape. One arm swung her way, but she deflected it. Another arm knocked the flashlight from Annie's cold fingers. She screamed.

Two big hands locked around her shoulders and threw her against the Dumpster. Ignoring the bruising pain, she shoved backward against her attacker, ramming her elbow into his gut. "Stop fighting," he muttered on a voiceless rasp.

"Nick!" she screamed.

But the man, much larger, much stronger, palmed the back of her head and shoved her forward. Her forehead connected with immovable steel, splitting open skin, numbing the point of impact. Annie collapsed to her knees as the darkness swirled around her and the snow rushed up to meet her. More scuffling noises buzzed through her foggy senses. The corner of the tarp broke free of its mooring and whipped against her.

And then she was jerked upward by the camera strap looped around her neck.

"No!" The thick strap strangled her and she instinctively scratched at the choking vise. The strap loosened for an instant and she latched on tight, holding on as he yanked her to her feet, trying to pull the camera from her neck.

"You crazy—"

"Hey. Hey!" Another voice was shouting, a man's voice. There was no mistaking the drum beat of running footsteps now. Or the deep shout of Nick Fensom's voice. "KCPD!"

All at once, the tension left the camera strap and Annie tumbled backward. She rolled onto her hands and knees and pushed herself up, snatching the swinging camera against her stomach as the dark figure ran toward the back of the alley.

"Stop where you— Damn it, Annie, get down!"

By the time she focused in on Nick's gun and re-alized she was in the line of fire, Nick had rushed past her. He charged through the alley like a line-backer chasing down the quarterback and disap-peared around the corner into the darkness. Both the attacker and her savior were gone.

Clear thoughts were still trying to work their way into her jumbled brain as Annie untangled the plastic tarp from her legs and staggered to her feet. A man had been hiding in the shadows, waiting to attack. How long had he been watching to make sure she was alone? Who was he? Why her? She was going to have plenty of bruises on her body, along with a crazy headache. She hugged her cam-era tightly to her chest.

The squeal of car tires spinning to find traction

and shouts in the distance diverted her thoughts to a different question. Had Nick Fensom really come to her rescue?

She was leaning against a brick wall, still puzzling out that last observation, when the detective in question came jogging back around the corner. The stocky shadow became a leather jacket and dark hair, blue eyes and stiff-lipped concern as he approached.

He tucked his gun into the back of his jeans as he spoke into the phone at his ear. "Track down those two cops and tell them to get their butts back here now. We've got a trespasser on the scene. Fensom out. Annie?" He stuffed the phone into his pocket and closed his hand around her arm. "CSI Hermann?"

"I'm okay."

But when he pulled her away from the wall and turned her, Annie's knees wobbled. Nick's face swirled out of focus and suddenly her feet left the ground. "Easy, slugger. I've got you."

She identified soft cold leather beneath her cheek before she realized that Nick had scooped her up in his arms and was carrying her out of the alley and along the sidewalk toward his silver Jeep. Annie's focus bounced along with every step, making her dizzy, and she squeezed her eyes shut. But other nerve endings were working just fine. The solid chest didn't move when she pushed against it. The muscular arms were locked firmly around her shoulders and knees.

"What are you doing? Where are you taking me?" What was happening to her? Nick Fensom couldn't annoy the hell out of her and then haul her around without some kind of explanation. She slitted her eyes open when the movement stopped. "You know, you've never once touched me before tonight, and now this is the second time you've gotten personal without my permis—"

Her butt hit the passenger seat of his Jeep as he set her inside. He reached across her lap and pointed to the radio on his dashboard. "Call it in to Dispatch. Lock the doors."

He hadn't even acknowledged her protest. Instead, he was pulling his gun again, retreating.

Annie grabbed a fistful of his jacket. "You're leaving me?"

"You said you were all right on your own." She'd lied. Yes, she knew how to be self-sufficient. Didn't mean she liked it. Especially when shadows came to life and attacked her. He laid his gloved hand over hers and gently pried it free. "Sit tight. I'll be back. I'm going to find out what the hell just happened."

"Nick—" But the door closed and he darted into the alley again. Falling snow and loneliness swallowed Annie up.

"WHERE DID GALBREATH AND Foster go?" Nick muttered out loud as he retraced the footprints he'd run past earlier before they disappeared beneath a fluffy layer of snow in the alley. Two sets besides his own went out, but only one came back into the alley. The perp who'd gone after Annie had waited there, by that trash can. Why hadn't the two uniformed officers gotten back to the scene ASAP? Or called him if they'd been delayed?

Nick stood at the edge of the curb where the north/south alley came out onto the street and looked up and down the block. With his gun still drawn and hanging down at his side, he took note of the green neon shamrock hanging in the bar window across the street a little ways down the block.

His instincts were to go over there and see if the missing officers had decided to ignore his emergency call and have an extra cup of coffee. He didn't know either man personally, but the only reasons a cop wouldn't answer a call for backup was because he was a lazy dumbass, he'd been disabled or he was on the take—and Nick wasn't comfortable with any of those options.

Nick's breathing quieted, but his suspicions mounted with every passing second. Something about this picture was all wrong. The street was too quiet. The hour might be late, but New Year's was a holiday that was about staying up all night and partying, especially in a trendy area like this downtown neighborhood. Yet there was not one person on the street besides him. No one waiting for a bus or cab or scraping off a windshield or darting through the shadows.

The man who'd attacked Annie was gone. And the two uniformed cops assigned to the crime scene weren't coming back.

Nick didn't like the answer he got from Dispatch when he called in to get the officers' location. "Relieved of duty? What do you mean they were relieved? By whom?"

"Officer Galbreath said Officer Gobel met them at the Shamrock Bar. Gobel and an Officer Ramirez were taking over the crime scene detail."

Nick swore. "Then put me through to Gobel and Ramirez."

A couple of minutes passed before the Dispatch operator came back on the line. Her apology was a bad, bad sign. "I'm sorry, Detective. Apparently, Officer Gobel is out of town on vacation. I have three Ramirezes on the personnel list—do you have a first name for me to contact?"

"No, forget it." If one cop was a fake, then he was guessing both men were impostors. He'd bet his next paycheck that one of them had come back to attack Annie while the other had waited close by to drive the getaway car. "Wait, do you have a twenty on Galbreath and Foster?"

"Yes, they're back at Fourth Precinct HQ."

"Good. Tell them to stay put until I call them." He had a traumatized CSI waiting for him back in his Jeep. He'd made a promise to his partner that he'd keep an eye on Annie Hermann and the crime scene—that he'd protect the task force and the work they were doing. He'd better turn around and do just that. With one last glance at the empty street, Nick headed back into the alley. "Call in a sketch artist, too. I want them to give me a good description of what this fake Officer Gobel looked like."

"I'll let them know. Dispatch out."

How had the two men gotten access to KCPD uniforms and IDs to look authentic enough to waltz into a cop bar and convince two legitimate officers to head back to HQ? How did they find out about the crime scene in the first place? Or were they after Annie? And why?

Nick wasn't going to find his answers here. His best bet was to get a description from the real officers and then run a facial recognition check through criminal databases and hope to get a hit on some real names. All that would take time. But right now, he needed to get back to Annie.

Decision made, Nick traded his gun for a flashlight and headed south toward the east/west alley. Because his gut was telling him he wasn't catching the perp in the black parka and ski mask tonight, he let his thoughts stray from the doorways and trash bins where he automatically checked for anyone hiding there. What was it about men in black parkas? First, Jordan Garza had put his paws all over his baby sister, and now one had assaulted Annie.

Or maybe it was the New Year that had brought out all the creepies and tilted Nick's world on its edge.

And what was the deal with Annie Hermann tonight anyway? Had he come to the crime scene with his concentration and emotions so out of whack over finding Nell making out with a gang-banger that he wasn't thinking straight? His concerns for his family had distracted him from the role he needed to play here. KCPD detective. Task force member. Protector. Period.

The Annie he knew had always been big mouth and attitude, not shy glances and vulnerability. She was Ivy League education and absentminded professor to his working-class street smarts and willingness to take point on the front line of the action. He teased her the way he teased his sisters. He respected her skills, got frustrated with her stubbornness and argued her out-of-left-field ideas. So there was no call for noticing how perfectly her small, dexterous hands had fit between his, or how her plain brown eyes turned a deep, soulful amber when she tilted them up at him and questioned why he was so eager to touch her tonight.

Man, he should be asking himself that same question. He needed a stiff drink or a good lay or a smack on the back of the head to get this ill-timed and inappropriate awareness of the woman—of the fact Annie Hermann *was* a woman and not some girl playing with her chemistry set—out of his head.

Nick turned the corner and collided with the distraction herself.

"Did you find Galbreath and the other officer?" She was sharp elbows and flashing eyes and tripping over one of his feet.

"Damn it, Hermann, I told you to stay in the car." He caught her by the arms to steady her and quickly release her, but she'd already latched on to the sleeve of his coat, denying him the clear-thinking distance he needed.

"It's been ten minutes."

"You're timing me?"

"I didn't know if something had happened to you." Her other hand was clutching the front of his coat now. "I didn't want to be alone. Even being with you is better than being alone right now."

"What you don't do for my ego." Casting aside the humbling revelation, Nick freed the leather from her death grip to turn her back toward the Jeep. "Come on. I don't think our perp's coming back. Neither are Galbreath and Foster."

He raised her fingers up to the illumination from his flashlight. She'd peeled off those sterile plastic gloves and replaced them with royal blue knit ones. But there was still blood on the fingers.

Her blood?

Nick swung the light up to her face, ignoring her squint as he brushed that wonderfully curly, dark brown hair off her forehead.

"What are you doing?" she protested, batting

his hand away. "What happened to Galbreath and Foster? Are they okay?"

Nick pushed back the edge of her blue stocking cap and cursed at the weeping gash at her temple. *Way to take care of people, Fensom.* The thickness of the wool and Annie's hair had probably saved her life. Answering the 9-1-1 pouring through his system, Nick mentally shifted gears. He hugged his arm around Annie's shoulders and hurried her through the alley. "That needs stitches. I have to get you to the E.R."

"But the officers—"

"Are gone. Some bogus cop calling himself Gobel met them at the Shamrock and sent them back to HQ."

"Fake cops?"

Nick nodded. "I'm guessing one of them attacked you."

"Why?"

"How the hell would I know? They didn't wait around to chat."

"And I never got a good look at him. All I saw were brown eyes. And he only spoke in a whisper. Nothing I could make out…" She kept pace with him for several yards. He gripped her arm tighter when they had to step over the flailing corner of a fallen tarp. When they reached the Dumpster where she'd found the victim's purse, Annie stumbled. She swayed back a step. And then she stopped.

She'd lost too much blood. She was passing out.

Halting in his tracks, Nick quickly unzipped his coat and shucked out of it. He draped it around her slender shoulders to add some warmth and stave off shock. But like his sister earlier that night, she shrugged it off. "Of all the stubborn…"

He saw the focus of her eyes and understood it wasn't stubbornness or bravado as much as something else had caught her attention. She lurched forward and Nick grabbed her arm to support her. She touched the pink, slushy smear on the brick wall where the blood had been. "He wiped away the handprints." She brought her glove back to her nose and made a face. Even Nick could smell the bleach from where he stood. "He's contaminated everything—cut the anchor ropes on the tarp. Snow's getting into…" She pulled away and dived into the pile of trash. "Oh, no." She tossed aside one bag, then two. "No, no, no, no."

"Annie." Nick slung his jacket around her again, looping his arm about her waist and lifting her away from the mess she was making. "We need to go. You're not thinking straight. We need to get you to the hospital."

"No." She spun in his grasp, fisted her fingers in the front of his sweater. "My kit is gone. He took my spare kit." She blinked away the snowflakes and blood from her upturned eyes. "Along with the evidence I'd gathered inside it."

Chapter Three

"It's just a cut, sir." Annie looked from the harsh scrutiny of her boss, Mac Taylor, the director of the KCPD crime lab, to the baffled expression of her friend and fellow CSI, Raj Kapoor, who lurked near the curtain separating this bay of the Truman Medical Center's E.R. from the other emergency treatment rooms. "Really, I'm okay."

Raj's black eyebrows came together like a fuzzy caterpillar when he frowned an apology. "You don't look so good to me, Annie." His accented voice conveyed both sympathy and surprise. "When Mac said you needed help at the crime scene, I thought he meant you couldn't carry everything in your kit."

Her kit. She let her head sink back into the pillow on the E.R. bay's exam table. Why would the rat who'd clobbered her steal her kit?

Her boss scowled behind the lenses of his glasses. He was so going to take her off this case if he believed she couldn't fix this mess.

Opening her eyes at the touch beneath her neck,

Annie looked for an ally in the friendlier countenance of the E.R. nurse who lifted Annie to wrap stretch adhesive around her head to anchor a protective gauze pad over the nine stitches in her hairline. "The doctor didn't seem to think it was anything serious, right?"

"I believe he mentioned concussion." The trauma nurse, whom Annie recognized from a couple of departmental social functions, was her supervisor's wife. Julia Dalton Taylor offered her a kind smile before reaching over to touch Mac's hand. "But trust me, I've seen a lot worse."

Even scarred by the accident that had cost him part of his vision, the stern look behind her boss's glasses melted for a second while he squeezed his wife's fingers. "You're in good hands, Annie." Then he turned the focus of his sighted eye back down to her. "I know some of the CSIs in my lab were cops before they became forensic investigators, but most of us are scientists—like you and Raj. I don't care if you are trained to use a gun, we're not supposed to go head-to-head with the bad guys out in the field." He leaned over her a moment, pulling aside the collar of Annie's sweater to inspect the bruise darkening around her throat, where the attacker had tried to yank the camera from her neck. "This shouldn't have happened."

"Mac." Julia shooed away her husband's hand and inquisitive concern. "She'll be fine."

With a pensive sigh, he adjusted his glasses at

his temple and pulled back. "When I got the call about your attack, the first thing I thought was that the Rose Red Rapist had returned to the scene to hurt you."

Interesting. Rumor—make that *legend*—around the crime lab was that Mac Taylor had earned those facial scars and lost the vision in one eye years earlier when *he* had gone head-to-head with some bad guys out to destroy the department's then-fledgling crime lab. Annie had a strong suspicion that she'd been the victim of something similar, albeit on a much smaller scale.

"The attack on me wasn't about rape, sir. This was…vandalism. Someone wanted to steal the evidence and erase any clues from the crime scene."

"From the sound of things, he did a thorough job."

Raj came over to the foot of the exam table. The caterpillar had separated into two eyebrows again. "I couldn't find the handprints you mentioned. Or any sign of your kit." He turned his dark eyes to their boss. "I did find bleach that had been splashed onto the bricks. Between that and the weather, the blood evidence Annie found has all been compromised."

"Raj, I want you to take those tarps and the cut ropes back to the lab. See if you can get any kind of trace off them, either from the original crimes or from Annie's attack. Maybe we can identify the tool that cut the ropes." Mac stepped aside as his wife moved in to finish doctoring Annie's wound. "It's not enough that this bastard won't get caught. Now he's messing with what little evidence we do have. I want to stay on top of this. I know it's a holiday, Raj, but I need you at the lab today."

"Of course, sir. I'll find whatever I can. Take care, Annie." Raj circled the table to take Annie's hand on the opposite side. He wrapped his dark-skinned fingers around hers and squeezed. "I'll see you soon."

"I'll be at work later today," she insisted, squeezing back. "Save something for me to do."

His dark eyes sparkled when he laughed. "You're a shameless workaholic, Annie."

She smiled back. "It's what I do."

Raj's phone rang and his smile vanished. He pulled the cell off his belt and checked the number. His eyebrows gathered in another frown.

Julia Dalton Taylor looked up from her work. "No cell phones in the E.R., please."

"I need to take this."

With a curt nod across the table, Mac dismissed Raj from the E.R. "Yes? I said I would. It's a holiday and we're short-staffed. You have to give me time…" Raj's voice grew more strident, his Indian accent more pronounced, as it faded into the hallway.

"I wonder what that was all about. He's right about one thing—we are short on help today." But when Mac looked down at Annie lying on the bed, his expression said he wanted to dismiss her, too.

"I'm so sorry." Annie's spirits faded beneath the bright lights shining down onto the E.R. gurney where she lay. Those tarps would be next to useless for retrieving any evidence; they'd been out in the elements for so long. There had to be a way to salvage this train wreck of a night. And then a memory surfaced in the pounding throb of her brain. "Wait. Call Raj back." She pushed herself up onto one elbow and pointed to the camera sticking out of her oversize purse on a chair in the corner of the treatment room. "I did manage to save the camera with all the shots I took of the crime scene. I'll show you." Swinging her legs over the edge of the gurney, Annie sat up to get it.

"Hold on, you're not going anywhere yet." With a hand on either shoulder, both Julia and Mac urged her to stay put. "I'll check it out."

Once he seemed convinced she'd sit still for Julia to complete her work, Mac borrowed a pair of sterile gloves from his wife's medical supplies and retrieved the camera himself.

Ignoring the headache that had been aggravated by the sudden movement, Annie still wanted to prove that she hadn't completely botched the investigation. "I can document everything he took, so we can put out a BOLO on the items that were in my spare kit."

Mac shook his head. "Even if we found them,

they'd be out of our chain of custody. Any findings would be inadmissible in court and any discoveries made from those tainted findings would be thrown out."

Annie knew that, but hope was about all she had left. This was a worst-case scenario for any criminologist, and if Rachel Dunbar's killer went free because Annie hadn't done her job, then she'd be disappointing all kinds of people—Mac Taylor, the crime lab, the task force, the D.A.'s office and KCPD—not to mention the Dunbar family. "Well, we still have whatever evidence comes off the victim. And I can go back with Raj to process anything that's left at the scene. Footprints, fibers from my attacker."

Mac offered her an apologetic smile. "It's been snowing out there for hours. Any trace evidence has been buried and degraded beyond usefulness. Raj already took anything we can process to the lab."

Hopeful thoughts faded and Annie's shoulders sagged. The clock on the wall above Mac's head said it was nearly time for breakfast. "The press has probably gotten wind of the theft by now. That'll give Gabriel Knight and Vanessa Owen plenty to criticize KCPD for in their reports. I'm sorry, sir."

"Quit apologizing." Mac opened up his own evidence kit and pulled out a bag to place the camera inside. "I'm more interested in the well-being of the people who work for me rather than a newspaper reporter with a grudge against the department or some spotlight-seeking woman and her camera crew." He locked down his kit and peeled off his gloves before facing her again. "I don't blame you for any of this, Annie. I'm mad because one of my people got hurt. Where's the officer who's supposed to watch over you while you process the crime scene?"

"Right here, sir." The curtain blocking off the room opened and her dark-haired annoyance-turned-rescuer appeared. "I assume it's all right to come in now, ma'am?"

What was Nick Fensom still doing here? She'd been in this examination bay for nearly two hours now. Once she'd filled out her paperwork and been called in to see a doctor, she assumed he'd gone back to chase down the bad guys, or at least knock on more doors and ask more questions and intrude on more New Year's Eve celebrations in the neighborhood where Rachel Dunbar's body had been found.

With a nod of permission from the nurse, Nick let the curtain close behind him and came farther in, filling up the tiny space with his heat and charging the cool, sterile air with that electric energy that seemed to follow him wherever he went. His blue eyes winced as they danced over Annie's bandaged head. Oh, great. First Raj and now Nick? Just how beat-up did she look? The grimace disappeared as he nodded to the trauma nurse. Then he turned his attention to the taller, older man bagging up her camera. "I'm Nick Fensom. Fourth Precinct. Your nephew, Pike Taylor, is on the task force with me." He thumbed over his shoulder to include Annie in the introduction. "With us."

"Mac Taylor, Crime Lab Supervisor." He slowly reached out to take Nick's extended hand. "This is your idea of teamwork? Maybe you'd better put Pike in charge of crime scene security, Detective."

Annie sat up a little straighter. True, Pike Taylor was a K-9 cop who specialized in security procedures, and whose height and bulk made up almost two of Nick. But the attack on her had been about stealth—Pike's brute strength wouldn't have kept her any safer than Nick's speedy response had.

"It wasn't Nick's fault," Annie explained. "I should have been more aware of my surroundings. I get a little obsessed when I'm working evidence and can forget the bigger picture. I should have called for backup as soon as I suspected there was someone in the alley with me. But I hesitated. I wanted to verify the intruder's presence first."

Nick's blue gaze nailed her over the bulge of his shoulder.

"You shouldn't have had to." Apparently, he didn't need or want her defense. His hand fisted in the thick leather jacket he held down at his side, his expression grimly apologetic as he faced the higher-ranking officer. "This is all on me, sir. I dropped the ball. I sent the uniformed officers away, and then got distracted by my own end of the investigation. I let her out of my sight for longer than I intended. It won't happen again."

"You won't let me out of your sight?"

"That's right. I intend to keep a close eye on you."

Annie puffed up at the implication she wasn't capable of taking care of herself. She pushed against the exam table. "I don't need a babysitter or a nurse." She flashed an apology to Julia Dalton Taylor. "Except for you, ma'am, of course. But I don't—"

"Relax, Hermann." Nick reached back and tapped her knee with the back of his fingers and she froze.

What was with all the touching tonight? This morning? Why were her traitorous nerve endings leaping to attention at even that most casual contact? Nothing had leaped when Raj had squeezed her hand. And who did Nick think he was anyway, deciding what she should or shouldn't do?

"Relax?" Impossible. But Nurse Taylor's hand on her arm diverted her attention, forcing her to be still while she cut and secured the last few inches of the bandage around her head.

Nick had already turned his attention back to Mac anyway. "If you need to write me up, sir, I understand."

Nothing about tonight was standard operating procedure in Annie's book. At last, she scooted off the edge of the table without anyone trying to stop her. When her feet hit the floor the room swayed a little and she grabbed on to the bed behind her and held on while her stomach righted itself.

"Whoa." Julia Dalton Taylor's hand was instantly there.

But Annie was tired of sitting and feeling weak and unable to take care of herself. "Why would he write you up? He's my supervisor, not yours. I'm the one who lost the evidence. *I* screwed up."

As soon as Nick spun around, he tossed his jacket over the end of the exam table and braced his hand beneath her elbow. "Are you seriously arguing with me about who gets to take the hit on their service record?"

Ignoring the zap of heat through her sweater sleeve, she shrugged his hand away and held on to Julia's arm until her legs steadied beneath her. "I'm saying I don't need a babysitter. I've never had a problem before tonight's call, and I damn sure won't ever let it happen again."

"Are you gonna take the next guy down all by yourself? Where was your gun?" Nick leaned in half a step. "Still in your car, right? Do you even know how to shoot the thing?"

Silently cursing her diminutive height, Annie tilted her head back and splayed her hand in the middle of Nick's chest to push him out of her personal space. "I was freezing cold and not thinking straight."

But the man didn't budge. Instead, she palmed a hard swell of muscle beneath the taut softness of the pale gray sweater he wore and her argument stuttered into silence. Nick wasn't the only one who'd overstepped the boundaries of professional distance and adversarial banter that normally described their relationship. She'd reached out to touch him more than once tonight, too.

There was a beat of silence in the E.R. bay, a moment frozen in time, before Nick spoke in a tight voice. "You shouldn't have gotten hurt, Annie. Not on my watch."

Her fingers tightened in the finely knit wool as the shadows of something mysterious darkened his eyes to a rich midnight blue. Her lips pursed to question him on the raw sound of that apology.

But before she could figure out exactly what she needed to ask, Julia circled behind Nick to stand in front of her husband.

"Mac, quit analyzing these two." Mac's quick snap of attention down to his wife made Annie realize her boss had been observing the interchange. She quickly snatched her hand away from Nick's chest and curled her tingling fingers into her palm. Just what had that clever eye seen? What was the deal between her and Nick this morning?

"She's my responsibility, Jules," Mac insisted. "I don't like it when my people get hurt. I feel I need to restrict her to the lab, where it's safe."

"No—"

"You know as well as I do that sometimes things happen that are beyond any one officer's control." Julia shushed Annie's protest and gently chided both men. "Instead of debating who's to blame for Miss Hermann's injuries, I'd be more worried about the two fake cops and what they said or did that convinced the legitimate officers it was safe to abandon their post."

Nick glanced back at the nurse. "I'm already working on that, ma'am."

Mac seemed to accept his wife's words more easily than Nick's or Annie's explanations and apologies. "I don't see the need for any kind of reprimand. Or restriction of duty. Yet." He pointed a finger at Nick. "But you keep an eye on her."

Nick's thick chest expanded with a deep breath. "Yes, sir."

Mac defused some of the tension between the two men by switching from supervisor to CSI mode. He dropped the camera into an evidence bag and scrawled his name on its chain-of-custody sheet. He brought it over for Annie to sign, as well. "I'll get this to the lab myself so we can get the pictures processed. I'll check it for the perp's prints, too."

"He was wearing gloves," Annie warned him. "I remember seeing black from head to toe—ski mask, hood, black parka, gloves—you won't find any identifiers."

Her boss was nothing if not thorough. "I'll check

it anyway. There could be trace. In the meantime, you get some rest." He turned to Nick. "You keep me in the loop on anything you find regarding Annie's assault. And you—" he dipped his sandy-blond head to kiss his wife "—I'll see at home."

Julia nodded, smiling up at her husband. "Happy New Year."

After Mac left, Nick picked up his jacket and shrugged into it. He pulled a charcoal-gray knitted scarf from his pocket and headed toward the curtain blocking them from the other E.R. bays while Annie turned her attention to Julia.

The nurse handed her papers and imparted some quick medical info. "The doctor left you this prescription for antibiotics, but with your tetanus shot current, there's really nothing you need to do except get some rest. If you develop a severe headache, double vision, nausea—anything that comes on suddenly and lingers or concerns you—call your personal physician immediately or come back to the E.R. Check in with your doctor in a week to ten days about removing the stitches. The information's all here if you have any questions. Do you have a ride home?"

Annie's mouth opened, but she didn't get a chance to speak.

"Yes, she does."

Annie swung around. Nick Fensom hadn't left. The crackle of electricity that blazed in those cobalt eyes hadn't gone, either.

He was daring her to argue with him. "I'm taking her home."

"All right, then. Off to the next patient." Julia gathered her instruments and computer pad. "Oh, and be careful about brushing your hair—those stitches will be pretty tender for a few days."

"I'll remember. Thank you."

With a friendly smile, the nurse left. There was no avoiding the burly detective now.

"I thought you'd gone." Nick's only response was to pick up Annie's black, knee-length coat off the chair beside him. "You don't have to take care of me."

He shook the coat open and held it up for her to put on. "Then you don't know me."

Maybe it was the bump on her head and exhaustion from being up all night, or maybe it was the unexpected glimpses of chivalry beneath Nick's thorny exterior that made her surrender to the cryptic promise she heard in his voice. Feeling too physically drained and off her mental game to put up any kind of fight, she simply nodded and turned to slide her arms into the lined wool sleeves.

If his hands lingered a moment to add another layer of warmth against her shoulders, Annie couldn't be sure. Nick pulled away as quickly as she'd imagined the tender gesture, muttering a choice word under his breath as he turned toward the sound of raised voices coming from the waiting room. Annie followed him out into the hallway where the commotion grew louder with every step.

He paused for a moment before turning the corner to the E.R.'s check-in desk. "Ah, nuts. Brace yourself."

"For what?" What she'd thought was an argument she could now tell were several excited people, all talking at once. "What is that?"

"My family." Nick squared his shoulders and moved forward again. "Mom. Dad."

"Nicky!" The group of people clamoring at the receptionist's counter turned as one and swarmed him. "Are you all right?"

The dark-haired man who answered to *Dad* reached him first. "George got a call that you were going to the E.R. Are you hurt?"

Butted aside by the flow of people surrounding Nick, Annie retreated to the wall to watch nearly a dozen concerned visitors hug him, squeeze his shoulder or shake his hand.

"I'm fine." Nick leaned in to kiss his mother's cheek. "In one piece. I promise."

His mother clutched her hand to her heart. "Thank God it was a false alarm."

"Then why are we at the hospital?" That was the silver-haired man in the dark green stadium coat.

"I had to bring a coworker in," Nick explained.

A petite woman with striking white hair went pale. "Not Spencer."

Nick chuckled. "Don't worry, Grandma, he's fine, too."

"Then who got hurt?"

"Annie..." Nick nudged aside a younger version of himself—a brother, no doubt—and spotted her shrinking away from the chaos. "Annie?"

"Oh, my goodness, look at her." At Grandma's pitying gasp, the swarm shifted course and moved toward Annie.

"I'm Connie."

The white-haired woman was quickly joined by Nick's mother. "Poor dear. I'm Trudy Fensom. Noah, get her a chair."

One of the brothers darted away. "I'm on it."

"What a bummer to spend your New Year's Eve in the hospital," a sister added, extending a hand to introduce herself. "I'm Natalie."

The family resemblance was strong in the Fensom family—dark hair, stocky shapes—the subtleties of maintaining a polite distance completely forgotten in their sudden concern for her. "I'm fine. Really."

"Come on, guys." Nick shouldered his way through to Annie's side. "Give her some room to breathe."

There were lots of introductions, strong handshakes and friendly greetings. She gave a quick rundown on what a criminologist did. And no, she'd never had stitches before. Did the bruise forming beneath the edge of the bandage really hurt? And then they were regaling her with past injuries, comparing if one sister's broken arm from a skiing mishap had hurt more than one brother's broken leg from a football collision.

In the span of a mere few minutes, there were conversations over conversations, and Annie lost track of more than one. She might have gotten the two brothers switched around. The names all started with N, right? Well, no, the mom's name was Trudy. The silver-haired man was Nicolas, Senior—but Nick's dad was Clay and Nick was the Junior. Or maybe Clay was a middle name and, oh heck.

"We haven't met." Annie startled at the hand on her elbow. She turned to see a distinguished-looking man in a cashmere sweater whose sharp gray eyes seemed faintly familiar. He pulled her a few steps away from the chaos and smiled. "I'm George Madigan. Nick's mother is my sister."

Annie snapped to attention. She wiped her palm on the black wool of her coat before shaking his hand. "Deputy Commissioner Madigan?"

"Guilty as charged." She glanced over her shoulder. Nick was taking the opportunity to herd his family to a less congested location out of the path of hospital staff for this early morning meet-and-greet. "You're Annabelle Hermann."

It was a statement, not a question.

Really? Nick was related to one of KCPD's top-ranking cops? He could have pulled rank if CSI

Supervisor Taylor had threatened him with a reprimand. And what connections did she have? Who was looking out for her in all of tonight's mess? Her eyes narrowed as she turned back to one of the department's senior command officers. "Am I in trouble?"

"Not at all. I oversee the budget for the task force among other things, so I'm familiar with all your names. But this isn't an official visit." He nodded toward the retreating group. "We all happened to be at Nick's house when my assistant called with the Dispatch report about an officer being hurt."

"And you thought it was Nick." That explained the crowd of Fensoms. "That must have scared you guys. I'm sorry."

"It's a hazard of being a cop, Annabelle. My ex-wife couldn't handle the risks involved, but Trudy's side of the family seems to take it all in stride."

That, they did. En masse.

"It's Annie, sir." The nerves that tightened her chest eased a little. The deputy commissioner's presence was just an uncomfortable coincidence, not a checkup on her inability to protect a crime scene. "No one calls me Annabelle anymore. Not since my folks passed."

"You lost them both?"

"Yes, sir. A car accident ten years ago."

"I'm sorry to hear that." He switched the coat he carried to the opposite arm and abruptly changed topics. "I'm assuming your assault is related to the

Rose Red Rapist investigation and I'll see a report on my desk in the next few days?"

Maybe this was some kind of off-duty check on the task force's progress, or lack thereof, with tonight's setback, after all. Annie wasn't sure exactly how the task force reports filtered up to the administrative offices of KCPD, but she was certain she'd be little more than a footnote at the next precinct chiefs' meeting with the commissioner. She'd better explain herself now. "I believe someone wanted to destroy evidence on the case, and I happened to be in the way of what he was after."

"Do you think it was our perp coming back to clean up the crime scene?"

"The Rose Red Rapist?" Would the man who'd been terrorizing the women of Kansas City for months now actually be bold enough to return to the scene of his crime? And possibly impersonate a cop to do it? The man they were after had been an enigma for so long, she'd just assumed he'd remain an anonymous threat in the shadows, and not risk any dealings with the authorities, whether perfectly disguised or not. "I don't know. I suppose it's a possibility, but I hate to speculate without more proof."

Which they no longer had. Annie wilted inside her coat.

"And all the evidence from Rachel Dunbar's murder is gone?"

"Everything but the body. And Mac talked to the M.E. who said her body had been—" she swallowed the bile the mere thought conjured "—sterilized like the previous victims."

"So we won't get much there," he concluded.

"No, sir. I did manage to save the pictures I took of the scene. Supervisor Taylor is processing those back at the lab."

"I see. Well, I'm glad your injuries weren't more serious." Just like that, George Madigan switched back to the friendly uncle again. "You have all your departmental insurance information?"

"Yes, sir. They took care of that when I checked in."

He smiled. "Good. And if you're a friend of Nick, it's Uncle George. When we're off duty, of course."

"Sir?" She wasn't a friend of Nick's, and she couldn't call the deputy commissioner by his first name.

He winked one of those gray eyes and laughed. "We'll work on that, shall we?"

When he crooked his elbow to escort her down the hallway, inviting her to rejoin the rest of Nick's chatty, outgoing family, Annie hesitated. If she couldn't handle Nick or his uncle one-on-one without her guard fully in place, then no way could she handle them all at once. Her breath caught in her chest and she buried her hands in the pockets of her coat and…

Her fingertips brushed against a pair of small plastic cylinders in the depths of her right pocket. Annie's toes curled inside her boots. The blood samples she'd taken off the alley wall were in her pocket. She still had evidence! The vials hadn't been in her kit, but technically, they'd never been out of her possession. A wave of reviving energy whooshed through her veins. Two small swabs of cotton weren't much to go on, but they were a whole lot more than she'd had a few seconds ago. She needed to call Mac Taylor and let him know they still had trace.

"Are you all right?" the deputy commissioner asked.

"Yes, I'm…" Annie pulled her hand from his arm and reached for her phone. She patted nothing but nubby wool. Where was her bag? "Excuse me a minute, um…" Annie frowned an apology. She couldn't bring herself to call him *Uncle George,* but she could drop the *sir.* "I forgot my purse. Excuse me."

Without waiting for a dismissal or a goodbye, she hurried back down the hallway into the exam bay where she'd gotten her stitches. Through the door, through the curtain—the friendly chatter of Fensom voices faded into white noise as she turned to retrieve her bag from the chair. Her lips buzzed with a big sigh of relief as she wrapped her hands around the pink paisley canvas and looped the long strap over her neck and shoulder.

And then she realized she wasn't alone.

Chapter Four

"They can be a bit much, can't they?"

Annie whirled around at the young voice. She grabbed on to the back of the chair and pressed her fingers to her temple as the room continued to spin. *Damn this bump on the head anyway.*

She squeezed her eyes shut, then blinked them open to bring the teenaged girl texting on her phone into focus. The dark brown color of her ponytail and the lavender hand-knit scarf wrapped inside the collar of her coat matched the colorful gathering of similar hand-knit scarves—lovingly made Christmas presents for each member of Nick's family, she'd guess—out in the waiting room. "You're part of Detective Fensom's family, too?"

The girl glanced up from the cell screen she was watching. "Nell Fensom. I'm Nick's baby sister. Guess you already met Natalie and Nadine."

"Nate and Noah, too. I'm Annie Hermann. I work with your brother." Annie barely noted familiar blue eyes before the young woman turned her attention back to the phone. Her thumbs flew

over the mini-keyboard. "Must be someone important this early in the morning."

"My boyfriend. Nicky KO'd seeing Jordan in
person last night, so we're keeping in touch this
way."

Although curiosity made her wonder why Nick
didn't approve of his sister's relationship, Annie
was anxious to get to her own phone and call Mac.
She waited politely for the pretty teen to finish her
texting and leave the room. "There sure are a lot
of you."

"I guess. Three boys, three girls, Mom and Dad,
Grandma and Grandpa, Uncle George. Plenty of
cousins, too." Nell typed in *X*'s and *O*'s, hit Send
and closed her phone before finally turning to
Annie. "How many are in your family?"

Just me. Unless she counted the cats. But it was
always so disheartening to share that. "I don't have
any brothers or sisters," she answered, telling the
truth without telling everything about her sad,
small life.

Nell's blue eyes widened. "You have your own
bedroom?"

As an only child, privacy had never been an issue
for Annie. "I have my own apartment."

"Sweet." Nell made a scoffing noise. "You're
lucky. Believe me, having five big brothers and
sisters can be a pain in the—"

"There you are." Nick barged into the tiny room.
"Thought we'd scared you off and you were sneak-

ing out the back way." His apologetic grin deepened into a frown when he saw Annie's company. "Nell, what are you doing in here?"

"Apparently not getting any privacy, am I." She rolled her eyes and sauntered past her brother. "Because this isn't a real emergency, can we go home now?"

Nick stopped his sister with a hand on her arm. "Why? Is Garza there waiting for you?"

"No." Nell twisted her arm free. "You scared him off."

Her phone beeped an alert and Nick's frown flattened into a grim line. "Are you talking to him?"

"Bye-bye." She waved her fingers over her shoulder, opening her phone as she waltzed into the hallway.

"Nell, you don't know how dangerous…" Nick took a step after her, but his legs locked up and his shoulders stiffened like concrete inside his jacket. Annie watched him rein in the frustration or anger or whatever emotion he was feeling before he turned back around. He swiped a hand over his dark hair, leaving it in a spiky disarray that matched the turbulence in his eyes and made her fingers itch to smooth it back into place. "Sorry about that."

"For what?" Annie puzzled at the emotions buffeting him. "She likes a boy—big brother doesn't. She seems like a normal teenager to me."

"If that's normal, I'm never having kids."

"You mean the large and in-charge Nick Fensom doesn't have the patience to deal with a teenager?"

"A saint doesn't have the patience to deal with that one. She's smart-mouthed and defiant—"

"And probably just as hardheaded as you." Annie wasn't sure where this defense of a girl she'd just met was coming from. Maybe it was just in her nature to argue with Nick. Or maybe some part of her could understand Nell's frustration in dealing with such an overprotective man. "She's probably trying to find her place in your family. I'd think it'd be easy to get overlooked with all those people. I'm guessing that having a boyfriend makes her feel special."

"What evidence are you analyzing now?" Nick taunted, drawing his shoulders back. "You've known her for all of two minutes. Nell's place is at home, not sneaking out to meet her gangbanger boyfriend."

Maybe Nick was right to be concerned. "He's in a gang?"

"She claims he's not anymore. But the kid's still got the look. He's got the car. He's got the 7 tat."

She'd worked plenty of crime scenes thanks to the 7th Street Snakes. The Latino gang was especially adept at jacking cars and selling drugs and dealing ruthlessly with anyone who stood in their way. "Have you checked this boy out? Does he know Nell's big brother is a cop?"

"He knows. Look, about the Garza kid…"

"That's her boyfriend?"

Nick nodded, then took a quick breath, as if he was about to say something more. But then he pressed his lips together and waved her toward the hallway. "Come on. I'll drive you home."

Annie tightened her grip around the strap of her purse. Although she understood Nick's concern about a 7 gang member dating his sister, she didn't like this acute awareness about all things Nick that seemed to have developed since the New Year had started. At least, she wasn't comfortable being so attuned to the man she'd called a pain in the posterior just a few hours earlier. Telephoning Mac offered the perfect excuse to make a polite escape from any more Fensom encounters. "You'd better go check on Nell. Besides, your family is waiting for you, and I need to make a phone call. I managed to save a couple of blood swabs from the Dunbar murder scene and I need to get them to Mac. Why don't you drive me to my car back at the crime scene instead? Then I can take the swabs to the lab to start processing them."

"You rescued some evidence?"

"Yes. From the bloody handprints. So it's important I get there sooner rather than later, and I don't want to inconvenience you any further." She gestured toward the door, meaning it with all sincerity when she said, "You have obligations."

Nick was already shaking his head. "Nurse Taylor said because of that concussion you weren't to get behind the wheel of a car for twenty-four hours. I'll take you to the lab. Then I'll drive you home and pick you up for work tomorrow morning."

"It's out of your way. I'll just call a cab."

"Out of my way? You don't even know where I live."

"Do you know where *I* live?" Why wouldn't he go away and leave her alone until she could get her head on straight? This stupid bump and stitches were messing with the logic that normally got her through her dealings with Nick. "It could take a while to run the tests. You've got all your family here, including the deputy commissioner. KCPD is already short-staffed. It's a holiday—"

"Did George say something to scare you? Threaten you with some kind of reprimand?" Hunching down, Nick's gaze drilled into hers. "He throws his weight around sometimes, but I'll straighten him out if he upset you."

"You don't 'straighten out' the deputy commissioner, even if he is a relative." Annie threw up her hands, desperate to have Nick understand just how uncomfortable this change in his behavior made her feel. She liked knowing where she stood with people—what they expected of her—what she could expect from them. Who was her friend? Who was her enemy? Who could she count on, and who was going to walk away when she needed him most? She could cope with independence and being alone. But she wasn't going to make a friend, or make something more, and then be crushed again. And she certainly wasn't about to put her trust in someone as confusing and unpredictable as Nick Fensom. "I'm tired and I want to go home, but I have work I need to get done first and I need my car to do that. If you really want to help, just do what I ask. If not, leave me alone so I can take care of what needs to be done myself."

"I'm trying to do the right thing here. I..." Just as another argument started, Nick pulled back. His chest, already far too broad and way too close, expanded with a deep breath. And then, before the instinct to put some space between them fully registered, he reached out to brush a curl away from the bandage on her forehead. A tiny shock of electricity sparked from his skin to hers at the unexpected caress and Annie's determination to get away short-circuited. "It's my fault you got hurt, so let me do this, okay?" His voice had dropped to a husky, mesmerizing pitch. "Let me play chauffeur for a day or two to make amends."

Her eyes locked onto Nick's as he studied the delicate movement of his fingertip, curling into a tendril of hair and pulling it gently away from her temple to tuck it behind her ear. He snickered when the tendril kinked back out of place and he determinedly repeated the effort.

He was touching her. Again. Ever so tenderly and...she liked it. Any urge to argue, to escape, vanished. She was back in that alley, with him rubbing her fingers and sheltering her from the cold wind, and her thinking just how masculine and protective and interesting the most incomprehensible man on the planet had suddenly become.

"It's nobody's fault…except for that…faceless creep with the big hands." Oh, great. Was that her voice stuttering through a whispered reassurance? "Mac and your uncle both planted the idea in my head that he could have been the rapist himself."

"Do you think it was that Rose Red bastard?"

He traced his fingertip around the shell of her ear, and a riot of goose bumps blossomed on the surface of her skin. Annie felt herself leaning into the caress. "I don't know. Even if we can get DNA or a blood type from the samples, there's nothing on file to compare them to. But maybe there's an accomplice we can identify. If those fake cops are the ones cleaning up after the rapist, then—"

"—we could bring them in and get them to turn on whoever hired them."

"We need to get something on this guy. Anything I can salvage from the crime scene helps, right?"

It was one reason the task force had been formed—after more than a dozen suspected rapes in almost as many years, the Rose Red Rapist had yet to leave any trace that could help identify him beyond the token rose he left with his victims. And the women he attacked from behind with a blow to the head could only describe a mask and a voice and the smell of the cleaning solutions he washed them with afterward. Nick understood how important even the smallest piece of evidence could be. "All the more reason I should have been there to protect you."

"If their goal was to retrieve something the rapist left behind, chances are they would have come back whether you were with me or not."

"Nobody comes after me. If I was there, you'd have been safe. We'd finally have something we could work with on this case."

"Don't be so arrogant." Annie reached up to wind her fingers around Nick's wrist. She found the warm beat of his pulse and pressed the pad of her thumb against it, wanting to soothe the guilt that tightened his features. "He was twice your size. Both of those men could have come back and outnumbered—"

"*Nobody* messes with me." The terse statement left no room for reasonable argument. "Or the things I care about."

Their hands froze in unison—his cupping the side of her face, hers clinging to the solid strength of his arm.

He cared about her? Annie couldn't quite process that. In the months they'd worked together, she and Nick had never done anything but argue. He was all about instincts and street connections—she was all about factual proof. Oil and water were never going to mix. She was still getting used to the idea that she found Nick attractive. Caring couldn't enter the picture yet.

Perhaps feeling the same sudden awkwardness she felt at this growing intimacy, Nick pulled away at the same time she did. But as she clung to the strap of her purse across her chest, Nick glanced over his shoulder toward the hallway behind him. Annie forced her brain to make proper sense of Nick's words and actions. *She* wasn't the one Nick cared about. Nick was worried about the investigation. And possibly his sister. "Is Nell in real danger?"

"He hasn't hurt her yet, or gotten her involved in anything illegal. But that doesn't mean he won't." Swagger returned to his posture and the contentious edge returned to his voice. "She says I'm overprotective. I don't know anything else but being a cop, and the guy I saw with his hands all over her raises every red flag in my book." He muttered a swearword before dialing his emotions back a notch. "Annie…I was on the phone with a friend of mine from the gang squad, checking up on this kid, when I heard you yelling for help. You and I are supposed to be on the same team, and I wasn't even working the case with you. I let you down. I should have known something was hinky when Galbreath and Foster didn't come back. I should have checked it out. On any other day I would have, but my head was somewhere else."

"You were worried about your sister. If I were in your place, I'd have been distracted, too."

"Don't make excuses for me."

"I don't make excuses. I look for explanations. There are always reasons why things happen the way they do—if we look hard enough." So his concern wasn't personal. The touching was all about guilt. And she'd been an idiot thinking for even one moment that there was some kind of personal connection here. Suddenly, logical arguments were easy to find. "We didn't know about the fake cops. We had no reason to suspect there was any danger. You didn't let me down." Nick was shaking his head, ready with more ammunition to make his point and accept the blame. "You chased the guy away before he could steal my camera or find the swabs in my pocket. You drove me to the hospital before I lost too much blood and got me the stitches I need so I won't be nicknamed Scarface."

"Scarface." Nick laughed and the atmosphere between them changed again. "That'd be a shame." He fought once more with the stubborn curl, brushing his finger across her skin. "It's a pretty face. I'd hate to see anything happen to it."

Pretty? Annie couldn't keep up anymore. Was he teasing? Flirting? Was this man her friend? Her enemy? A coworker? Something more? She had to ask. "What's going on between us here, Nick? I'm confused, and I don't like it when I don't have answers."

"If I figure it out, I'll let you know." She wasn't sure if it was reassuring or disconcerting to learn that Nick didn't understand this weird chemistry that had developed over the past six hours, either.

And then, with a deep exhale that fluttered across her cheek like long-suffering resignation, Nick leaned in and pressed his lips against hers. For one startled moment, Annie froze. Her eyes opened wide, tilting up to seek his. But then his fingers tunneled ever so gently into her hair and he drifted closer, urging her head back, demanding a response.

Her eyes shuttered at the curious intent of his lips moving over hers, coaxing her to give in to the taste of his tongue sliding across the seam of her mouth. Daring her to ignore the electricity of the charged air that separated their bodies by mere inches. Inviting her to join him in this little bit of crazy.

Annie's surrender was slow in coming, but surprisingly eager once the walls of logic and routine guarding her actions crumbled and an answering desire surged through her blood. Her fingers curled into the buttery-soft leather of Nick's jacket, and her mouth softened to cling to the firm heat of his kiss.

Random observations flowed through her senses and imprinted on the brain cells inside her head—coffee and sweet cake flavored his tongue. His lips were supple, masculine, thorough. The stubble that rasped against her skin was prickly soft and scented like crisp winter air and earthy heat.

She hadn't kissed a man since the debacle of Adam dumping her. And she'd never been kissed with the raw, driving need that powered Nick Fensom's kiss. She wasn't sure how to answer that kind of potent emotion other than to hold on with both hands and answer every exploration of his tongue, every press of his lips, every breath, every pulse beat. Her hips hit the table behind her. The floor swirled beneath her feet. His heat swallowed her up.

This was all too fast. Too much. Totally wrong.

His hand slid behind her waist, anchoring the swell of her bottom as his thighs butted into hers. A guttural noise hummed in her throat as Nick's chest rubbed against hers, seeking contact through the layers of coats and clothing they wore. The tips of her breasts sprang to attention. Arrows of fire zinged through her body from his chest to his fingers to his lips and everywhere in between. She'd never felt this aware. This alive. This right.

His fingers tightened against her scalp, accidentally tugging her hair.

"Ow."

"I'm sorry." He shifted both hands to cup her face, taking another kiss between each apology. "Sorry. So sorry."

But the sharp jab of pain beneath her bandage was the wake-up call Annie needed. Her murky thoughts cleared as though an overhang of snow had just plopped inside the collar of her coat.

Kissing Nick Fensom—kissing anyone like

this—was completely out of character for her. And a huge mistake on so many levels.

She pushed with the fists bunched in the front of his jacket, opened her eyes—both literally and figuratively—and dropped her chin to pull her mouth from his. *Stop.* The plea stuck in her parched throat. Her reaction made no practical sense. She was grappling with Nick in a tiny hospital exam room the same way Roy and his girl friend du jour had been ringing in the New Year outside her apartment door. And they'd been drunk.

Annie knew better.

"Nick…" *Oh, snap.* Yes, that breathless gasp had come from her throat. Since when did she do *breathless?* What kind of sense did that make—to forgo reason and slip so far out of control? She made such an easy mark for future awkwardness, hurt and humiliation. Pride gave her a little bit of backbone. Remembered abandonment and disappointments gave her something more. Annie tilted her face to Nick. "What was that?"

His chest heaved in and out as he spread his arms out to either side, stepping back as if he'd been called on some kind of charging-into-personal-space foul. "A kiss?" His gaze zeroed in on her parted lips and silent pants, perhaps assessing her reaction. "What did you think it was?"

Some subconscious part of her brain must have broadcast encouragement because he shifted his stance and leaned in again. But that impulsive part of her brain didn't get to be in charge. Not for long. And neither did Nick. With a resolute huff that denied him any further welcome, she palmed the center of his chest and pushed him firmly away. Annie needed cool air between them, room to think and prioritize.

"I'm asking *why*. For months now we've barely gotten along at work, and now you..."

"Seriously? You can turn it on and off just like that?" He raked his fingers through his hair, turning away, then facing her again. "You ask too many questions."

"You kissed me out of guilt. Or you needed consoling because you were worried about your sister."

"Consoling?"

"Stress makes people do things they normally wouldn't. It could have been leftover adrenaline or..." She swallowed her next hypothesis and concentrated on what was really important here. Whatever was behind that kiss didn't matter. "I need to get to the lab. So if you want to help me—"

"The men you date must be gluttons for punishment."

"I don't date. I don't make out like some kind of hormonally charged teenager with a man I can't stand, either."

"Can't stand?" With a deliberate flick of his wrists, Nick smoothed out his jacket where she'd crushed it in her fists. "You seemed to like me well enough a second ago."

"I work." Ignoring the obvious, uncomfortable proof of her willing participation in that embrace, Annie tried to reestablish order in her world. "I focus on my work. I get results. I find answers. I *need* answers."

He propped his hands on his hips, assuming the adversarial stance she was more familiar with. "All work and no play? Sounds lonely."

He had no idea. But at least she wasn't hurting the way she had a year earlier, or even ten years ago when her parents had died. "Nick, that can't happen again. We have a job to do. You have to promise."

With unblinking intensity, those blue eyes studied every nuance of her expression. Annie curled her fingers around her bag, fighting the urge to look away from the probing assessment.

"You are some piece of work, Annie Hermann. A lot more complicated than anything I'm used to." And then, for some inexplicable reason, he grinned. "Keeps me on my toes, I guess." The sudden lightness in his expression was so surprising that she didn't immediately protest when he pried her fingers from her purse. Wrapping his hand around hers, he pulled her toward the hallway. "Let's go run the gauntlet."

"Your family?"

"I heard my mom and grandma mention something about chicken soup."

"For me?" Annie stopped in her tracks, pulling her hand free. The Fensom family was Nick times ten. And he was more than enough for her solitary self to deal with right now.

Nick turned with a weary sigh. "Is friendly concern against your scientific principles, too? You know, sometimes people just do what feels right. They don't stop to calculate how it's going to affect the future. My family's like that. They're good people."

"I wasn't insulting them. But we just met. They don't even know me."

"Call it guilt by association. If I'm taking care of you, they'll want to help, too."

"Why?"

"Damn it, woman…" His hands sliced through the air, emphasizing the frustration in his tone. "There isn't always a reason. It's just what families do. They support each other."

"I'm not family."

The frank, unadorned statement halted the handspeak and softened his expression. "If I promise not to let them all show up on your doorstep at the same time, will you stop arguing every little thing and just let me take you home?"

"To the lab," she corrected him.

His shoulders deflated with a weary sigh. But those blue eyes were smiling. "Right. I'm driving you to the lab. Come on, slugger."

This time, he didn't try to take her hand. Instead, he shortened his stride to walk beside her into the hospital's waiting room. And as the greeting and concern of Nick's family swarmed around them again, Annie was painfully aware that while he offered her the support of a comrade-in-arms, he'd never made that promise not to kiss her again.

Chapter Five

"Are you sure you want to chauffeur me around for another twenty-four hours? Maybe you need to check in on your sister. You haven't seen your family all day. Or eaten a meal."

Seriously? She was going to try that cutesy schtick on him now? Nick shifted the Jeep into Park, ignoring Annie's winsome smile. Ceaseless debate hadn't gotten rid of him at the hospital or the crime lab, and feminine charm wasn't going to dissuade him now.

"You asking me out to dinner?"

"No."

"Do you have a car to get to work in the morning?"

"No, but that's because you wouldn't take me to mine." She pointed to the brownstone apartments across the street. "You know, once I'm inside, I can still call a cab and go get my car after you leave."

"No, you won't."

Annie muttered something distinctly unfeminine and sank back in her seat. "You *are* leaving, right?"

Nick leaned back in the heated seat, surveying the fenced-in parking lot with its empty guard booth and security gate where he'd swiped her resident card to raise the plastic guardrail that was more about privacy than protection. Frustration radiated off her in waves at his silence, and Nick grinned. If she hadn't learned yet what a stubborn son of a gun he was, she'd understand soon enough.

The light at the far end of the lot flickered on and off with the gusting night wind, and the streetlamps outside the lot were spaced far enough apart that they left plenty of shadows where a perp could scale the fence without being seen to jack a car, do some vandalism or commit an even more personal crime. He'd be on some landlord's case about standard safety expectations if any of his sisters lived here.

The smile was back when she tried to reason him out of his protective penance again. "You said you live over near Raytown. No way is this a convenient drive from there."

He scrubbed his hand over his jaw and watched the flakes of snow gather on his windshield where they melted and ran down to pool against the wipers. He was bone tired, in sore need of a shave and in no mood to go another verbal round with Annie. But the woman wouldn't quit.

"I can take Blue Ridge Cutoff by the stadium and get home in no time. It's not like there'll be any baseball games there this time of year to back up traffic." He thought she'd been mulling over the crime scene pictures she'd copied at the lab once Mac Taylor had cleared her camera and pulled the memory card for her. But maybe she'd spent the last twenty minutes of the drive across town cooking up ways to get him out of her personal space. Like that was going to happen. "Besides, you're downtown, practically at the back door of precinct headquarters here. Once I pick you up in the morning, the drive to work will take us no time."

Did she just roll those amber eyes? His sister Nell had an irritating penchant for doing that. But Nick couldn't recall ever being this aware of his sister's eyes. Annie's were darker now, like a fine whiskey. Did she even know how their color changed, from light golden hazel to nearly brown, according to her mood? And why did *he* know that? He was beginning to think the sparks that had been flying between them for months now—since being assigned to the same task force—had more to do with some sort of dormant attraction that was waking, despite his best efforts, than it did with any differences in their personalities or investigative styles.

Annie's scent filled up the closed space of the car—a mix of antiseptic from the lab and something more subtle, like lavender and vanilla, that stirred the air with every bounce of those dark, velvety curls. He was a damn fool for noticing all those little feminine details about the eccentric scientist. This crazy pull to the woman stewing in

the seat across from him could become as dangerous a distraction as his worry over Jordan Garza
dating his sister.

And while Nick had made the mistake of letting
personal feelings get in the way of doing his job
once already today, he wasn't about to make that
mistake a second time. No matter how the complex,
combative brunette got under his skin and messed
with his head, he was determined to watch over her.

With that much of a New Year's resolution firmly
in place, Nick turned off the engine and opened the
door to let a blast of frigid air swirl in to cleanse
Annie's fragrance from his car and his senses.

Tightening the scarf his mother had knitted him
for Christmas around his neck, Nick hunched his
shoulders against the cold and circled the car. Before he could reach her side, Annie was already
out, opening the back door to retrieve the new evidence kit she'd brought home from the crime lab.
Next thing he knew, she was striding toward the
exit gate.

Nick locked up the Jeep and hurried to catch up.
"Where are you going so fast?"

"Um, home?" She trudged through the ankle-
deep snow gathering on the sidewalk. "Thanks for
dropping me off. See you in the morning. Good
night."

He plucked the boxy black case from her hand
and wrapped his fingers around her upper arm.
"I'll walk you in."

"Give me that." Although she tugged against his grip, Nick's hand didn't budge. "The doctor didn't say anything about my not being able to walk."

"I want to get a look at your place, see what kind of security you've got." He paused to look both ways along the vehicle-lined street before plunging into the snow that drifted against the curb. It was an old habit of his from his tenure working gang enforcement to count cars and make a quick scan of models and colors. That's when he noticed the two men sitting in the black SUV half a block away. "Hell of a cold night to spend it waiting in a car."

"Then go home where it's warm. May I have my kit, please?"

He tipped his head toward the SUV. "I'm talking about those guys. Do you know them?"

She leaned forward to peek around him. "I don't think so. But it's too dark to get a good look at their faces."

"That's why you need more lights around here," he muttered. "What about the car?"

"It doesn't look familiar. But then, I don't know everyone in the neighborhood." Suddenly, her fingers had glommed onto the sleeve of his jacket. "You don't think it's him, do you? The man from the alley? Did he and his partner follow us?"

Nick eased the death grip on his sleeve and pulled her into step beside him to cross the street. "No."

"Are you sure?"

"Yes, I'm sure. While you were busy thinking up ways to get rid of me, I was watching the traffic. No black SUV on our tail."

"Then it's probably just a coincidence that he's here, right?" Nick didn't like coincidences. "Right?"

"You need to be more aware of your surroundings," he advised, forcing her shorter legs to hustle a little faster. "Don't stand around analyzing things. That gives anyone watching you the same time to observe your actions and plan their strategy. Make quick impressions and keep moving."

"Analyzing things is what I do."

"In the lab, but not when it involves personal safety." Unsure whether the men were simply waiting for their car to warm up before driving it, or if they were up to something more sinister by lurking in the shadows, Nick tried to make out a plate number he could call in. No good. He'd have to come back out and check on the SUV once Annie was secure in her apartment. "I suppose if the lot's full, you park out here on the street and walk past all these cars?"

"Aren't you being a little paranoid? I was perfectly safe in the lab all day, even without your pacing the hallways, asking coworkers to identify themselves and making them nervous."

"Besides you and Mac Taylor, I saw three people in that whole building today. Raj Kapoor who brought in the tarps from the alley and processed them with you, the guy finishing up paperwork in his office on the fourth floor and the guard at the front desk. That's another thing—there's safety in numbers. I know you like that whole leave-me-alone-and-let-me-do-my-work thing, but you make less of a target if you've got some backup with you."

"Why would I be a target?"

"Let's see. You've been attacked once already—"

"That man was stealing evidence. It wasn't about me."

"You're a successful professional. The type of woman the Rose Red Rapist targets. Maybe you should watch out for him." To date, their unsub hadn't discriminated in looks or ethnicity when choosing his victims. The common denominator seemed to be his penchant for brutalizing strong women—and this one's obstinate will certainly qualified her.

Snowplow crews had been through here at least once in the past few hours to clear the street, creating deep snowbanks around the cars that hadn't been moved since the winter storm had begun before the New Year last night. Nick stomped a path through a drift to reach the curb, feeling the snow cling to his jeans and chill his legs. He kicked aside the tiny avalanche that spilled onto the sidewalk and turned back to reach for Annie's hand. "Watch your step."

Despite the murderous glare in her eyes, Annie was practical enough to fold her fingers into his, holding on for balance while she made the precarious climb to the sidewalk. "This is the wrong place for him," she reasoned. "He likes the uptown district where all the outsiders are pouring in their money to revitalize the historic buildings and bring back the neighborhood. Besides, he went after Rachel Dunbar last night. It's not his pattern to strike again so soon."

"His pattern changed when Dunbar died. Who knows when he'll strike again."

She paused in the middle of the snowbank. The defiance in her tone was replaced by something softer that matched the concern in her eyes. "Not every person you run into is a threat, Nick."

"Maybe not, but I don't want to miss the one guy who is because I wasn't paying attention."

Her right foot slipped on the ice compacted beneath the snow and Nick tightened his grip. He was pulling her over the slick mini-mountain when he heard a big engine revving.

Nick's gaze flew to the black SUV. Tires squealed against the pavement, fighting for traction. "Move!"

The CSI kit sank into the snow. Nick cinched his arm around Annie's waist. She yelped as he lifted her off her feet and spun around, setting her on the sidewalk behind him. The driver opened up the throttle and the black car fishtailed onto the snow-packed road, spitting up a spray of slush, ice and road salt as it barreled toward them.

"You crazy—"

Annie's shout muffled against Nick's chest. He covered his face with one arm, squinting against the pelting debris, turning his shoulders to protect her from the worst of the deluge—all the while trying to get a glimpse of a face or a plate number or any identifying mark that could help him track the jerk as soon as he got on the phone to Dispatch. Ice chips stung his face and stuck to his clothes. The slush soaked through wool and leather, straight through to the skin.

"Stay put!" Nick pushed Annie back behind the protection of a parked car and charged after the speeding vehicle. Black. Souped-up engine. Missouri plates, he noted, but little more. It was three blocks away, gaining speed and disappearing into the night before he even made it to the corner.

"Son of a—" Nick skidded to a stop, swinging his gaze back and forth to make sure there were no more unwelcome surprises waiting for them. He dropped his jaw open, exhaling deep foggy breaths after the quick sprint through the frozen night.

"E-14."

"What?" He spun around to meet the dark-haired beauty running up behind him. "Damn it, Annie, why didn't you stay put?"

He caught her by the shoulders, moving her farther away from the intersection, away from the street and beyond any other spy's line of sight. She was slightly winded and fumbling with her purse and camera, but that tongue of hers worked just fine. "I couldn't see the license plate over the roofs of the parked cars, but I could make out a parking sticker on the back window. I couldn't read where the lot was, but saw *E-14*." She got a firm hold of the camera and held it up like a winning trophy. "I got pictures. If there was enough light on even one of them, I can blow it up and read the fine print, maybe get the license number."

"Annie." She'd done all that in the few seconds he'd given chase? Why hadn't she just dropped for cover? Those could have been bullets flying at them instead of sooty snow and ice. Dropping his arm around her shoulders, he tucked her to his side and scooted her back toward the apartment complex. His eyes were watching every car, every window they passed, whether they showed signs of life inside or not. "When I tell you to do something, you need to do it."

The woman planted her feet, nearly toppling over when Nick didn't immediately stop. Her hand latched on to him, squeezing melting slush from his jacket and scarf through her bare fingers. "You told me not to just stand there and analyze."

"There's a difference between..." Not wanting to stand out here in the open any longer than they had to, he nipped that argument in the bud, conceding her point—and admiring that she'd thought so quickly on her feet. "I did, didn't I? Figures you'd decide to listen to me now. Good work."

"Thanks." Oh, man, was he in trouble. She was

too pretty when she smiled like that. The flat-out worry that had tightened his chest eased with that cautious little smile and he felt the corners of his own mouth crooking in response.

But knowing his first move shouldn't be to come up with some other compliment to keep her smiling, Nick pulled her hand away from his wet leather and dripping scarf. Sparing a few seconds to wipe the moisture from her pale fingers and slide his gloves from his hands onto hers, he ignored the chill on his own skin and pulled her back into step beside him. "Come on. Let's get you inside before you freeze."

"You're the one who's freezing. I'll put on a pot of coffee. I have to get you out of those wet clothes."

Nick stopped to close the kit she'd thrown open, ignoring the sudden warming beneath his chilled skin at the suggestive invitation of that one innocent line. A completely naughty image of Annie Hermann stripping off his clothes made him forget the weather entirely for a few awkward seconds. Would the bedroom Annie be the single-minded, precisely adept scientist he'd watched working in the lab all day? Or would she be the softly vulnerable klutz in the hospital E.R. who held on with both fists and kissed him with guileless abandon?

Practicality cut the fantasy short. They were still out in the open, and if the guys in the black SUV *had* been watching for Annie's arrival, then anyone else could just as easily be watching them from the

shadows. He hooked her elbow and starting walking into the courtyard framed on three sides by
the two-story brownstones. "Coffee sounds perfect right about now."

"I'll even throw in a sandwich or an omelet,"
Annie offered, taking him to a more familiar place.
Coworkers. Brainy lady and bodyguard. Crazies out
there in the world who'd hurt her once, had nearly
hurt her a second time and who wouldn't get the
chance to hurt her again.

"I get it. Now your strategy is to poison me so
you can get rid of me."

"It's an option," she teased, and Nick chuckled
in his throat. This back-and-forth banter was definitely more familiar than the magnetic spell she'd
cast over him today and very real concerns he had
for her safety. "I'm starting to see how you might
be useful to have around for a while."

"I must have snow in my ears. That sounded like
you just said something nice to me."

She stopped on the front steps at the first building, and pulled the security card out of her pocket.
She tilted her face to his, showing him something
far too vulnerable and dangerously distracting in
those soulful eyes. "I slipped on the ice and was
on my way down to the pavement. Whether that
SUV was just an idiot driver who can't handle this
weather, or it was something intentional, I would
have fallen into the street, right into his path if you
hadn't been here. Thank you. Again."

Nick took the card from her hand, giving her fingers a reassuring squeeze before swiping the card to open the door and usher her inside. "Don't think this makes us even, Hermann. I'm still going to look after you for the next forty-eight to seventy-two hours. Just like the doctor said."

"Twenty-four hours, max."

He waited for the door to close behind them, then followed her up the steps to the second-floor landing. "You can't get rid of me."

"I still want my car."

"Ain't gonna happen."

She'd pulled out her keys by the time he reached the top step. He was glad to see she had to unlock a dead bolt in the thick walnut door as well as the knob. While the security outside hadn't been all it should be, it was reassuring to see things improving inside the building.

Or not.

The door on the opposite side of the landing swung open and a big man with a TV remote clutched in his hand joined them. "Annie? I was watching the game, but I thought I heard you coming in. Are you okay?"

She muttered something like *"Not now"* before turning with a smile. "Hi, Roy. I—"

Stifling her greeting, the man walked straight over to Annie and lifted her onto her toes in a hug. Something hot and protective jarred through Nick's cold body at the man's presumptive right to put his hands on her. She clearly knew the guy, but was this a neighbor? A friend? Something more?

Something worse?

"I was worried. When I took Betsy home this morning, I saw you were still gone. You left last night and you've been gone all day—" Just as Nick reached out to separate them, the man set Annie down and pulled away. His gaze zeroed in on the violet-and-purple swelling above her left eye. "Oh, man, you're not okay." The shoulders of the red football jersey he wore puffed up, and Nick saw his stance shift. "Did this guy do this to you?"

As soon as the guy thumped Nick's chest, Nick grabbed his hand, twisted his arm behind his back and pushed his face up against the wall. "I'm KCPD, pal. Who are you?"

"Roy Carvello, neighborhood watch." The remote clattered to the floor as his cheek rubbed against the plaster. "It's my duty to check on her."

"It's okay, Roy. He never hurt me. Nick, let him go." A gentle hand squeezed around Nick's shoulder, shooting a tiny jolt of electric awareness through him.

"You said, 'Not now.' He grabbed you anyway."

"I'm just tired. I'm not used to dealing with so many people all day long. Please." More than the guy's free hand raised in surrender, Annie's touch and soft voice cut through the blinding frustration of yet another attempt to keep her safe gone wrong. Nick eased his grip and slowly backed away, giving Roy Carvello room to turn around. Annie's hand curled through the crook of Nick's elbow, pulling him back another step. "Detective Fensom's okay. He's…" Her grip pulsed around his arm. "He's a guy I work with. He gave me a ride home because I couldn't drive."

A guy I work with? Their relationship had gotten a lot more complicated than that over the past twenty-four hours. How did she explain that kiss at the hospital? Clinging to him for protection and comfort? What about the way their endlessly argumentative banter had changed to teasing quips and grins and friendly intimacy in just the last few minutes?

He'd stopped being just a guy she worked with sometime between carrying her out of that alleyway and accepting her invitation for food and coffee.

Nick was a tangled-up mess inside, going on thirty-six hours without sleep, dealing with guilt, fighting his own hormones and on guard against any man until they could ID her attacker. He knew the perp would come back to finish what he'd started. And she was shootin' the breeze with Tall, Dark and Nosy here?

Carvello straightened the jersey he'd put on over a black hoodie and jeans. "Isn't there some law against police harassment?"

He'd thrown the taunt at Nick, but it was Annie

who answered. "It's been a long day, Roy. Detective Fensom is a little overprotective of me."

"What's wrong with your car?" Roy asked. Turning his eyes to the petite brunette, his accusatory tone eased back into friendly concern. "Were you in an accident?"

"My car's fine. It's parked downtown." She released Nick to point to the bandage above the bruise. "I got this bump on my head and the doctor doesn't want me to drive. How was your party? Looks like you and Betsy were having a good time." Annie tilted her head to peek into his open apartment. "She didn't stay for the game?"

"No. She helped me clean up the place. Then I took her to breakfast and drove her home." Roy reached out to touch Annie again, but a warning look from Nick forced his hand back to his side. "Who did that to you?"

"That's a crime we're trying to solve."

"You look like you've been in the boxing ring for a few rounds." He thumbed over his shoulder into his tidy apartment. "Do you need anything? I've got an ice pack. Aspirin. Leftover pizza. A private phone you can use?"

"I'm okay."

Did this bozo really think Nick had hurt Annie? "We appreciate your concern, Mr. Carvello, but I've got it covered."

"Yes, sir, Officer." Roy dropped his gaze to the puddle around Nick's feet. "Dude, you're dripping on the floor. The landlord refinished these last summer. He won't like that you're making a mess."

Nick opened his mouth to mention snowstorms and ice and the jackass who'd nearly plowed into Annie. But her hand was on his arm again, cutting through the tension, calming him down. She picked up the remote and slipped it into Carvello's hand. "It's okay. I'll get a mop and clean it up."

"I'll do it for you. It can't stay there for long or it'll pull up the finish. It's halftime anyway. You just go get into some dry clothes and let me take care of it."

"That'd be a great help, Roy. Thanks. Good night."

Her smile was contagious. "Good night, Annie."

But once they were inside her apartment, the smile vanished and Annie turned on him. "What was that?"

"What was what?" While she unbuttoned her coat and unzipped her boots, Nick locked everything.

Her boots thumped down on the throw rug beneath his feet. "That Neanderthal reaction to my neighbor looking out for me?"

Nick paused with his hand on the chain that added another layer of security. What was that knee-jerk reaction to Roy Carvello wanting to touch Annie all about anyway? Protective instincts? Or jealousy? It better damn well not be the latter, or else his ability to watch over Annie the way he needed to would be in serious trouble. He hooked the chain and faced her. "Did I interpret that wrong? Did I not see you cringe when Carvello opened his door? Remember, I'm not waiting to be blindsided by the one guy who *is* a threat."

"Okay, so Roy doesn't understand boundaries." She hung her coat on the rack beside the door and indicated he do the same. "But he's not a bad guy. He keeps an eye on things when I'm gone."

"Why didn't you want him to touch you?"

"Because I'm happy being friends and he wants... How did you know?"

Nick tapped the badge hanging at the center of his chest. "Detective?"

With a heavy sigh, she knelt down to cuff the hem of her jeans above her stockinged feet. "He wants to be more than that. Well, actually, I think he wants to be more than that with every woman he meets. I had to fend off his advances once when he was drunk."

"So he's a player."

Annie stood, still defending the guy. "Sober, he's a good neighbor."

"I don't like him. And I don't think you like him much, either."

"How would you know? You've known him for only five minutes, and you spent half that time with your forearm pressed against the back of his neck."

"Then he shouldn't have touched you."

"Look, I don't have that many friends around

here, so I'd appreciate it if you wouldn't alienate the one guy…" She worked her rosy pink lips between her teeth, stopping the argument. Before continuing, she plucked his stained, dripping scarf from his hands and carried it into her galley-style kitchen where she rinsed and squeezed it dry in the sink. "Coffee, sandwiches and dry clothes, remember? I owe you that much."

"You owe me nothing."

"Don't you ever get tired of fighting with me?" She circled the counter into the hallway and pulled out a towel to wrap up his scarf. She tossed him a second towel and pointed to the radiator beside the front windows. "You can warm yourself over there while I change and come up with something for you to wear. And don't scare my cats the way you scared Roy."

"You have cats?" Right on cue, a brown-and-cream Siamese slinked out from under her sofa and rubbed himself against Nick's ankles. Roy Carvello had been just as bold, just as determined to touch. The big guy across the hall hadn't been scared. If anything, he'd been angry, defiant, when Nick had intervened. The way he'd touched Annie… And he'd done more than that when he was drunk? Yeah, he'd better look a little more closely at that jealousy thing. "I'm sorry if I overstepped the line between friends. Coworkers," he clarified.

But she'd already marched down the hallway and closed the bathroom door behind her.

"Yeah." Nick knelt down to stroke the cat between the ears and make his confession to it. "So, between you and me, I'm tired of fighting, too."

Chapter Six

Fortified by a quick shower, her gray sweats and a toasty warm pair of hot-pink slipper socks, Annie pulled her father's red plaid flannel shirt out of her keepsake drawer and carried it down the hallway to the living room. She stopped at the end of the hall, hugging the soft shirt to her chest. She wasn't sure if it was the sight of Nick's broad, naked back, tapering down to the belt on his jeans, the cat curled around his bare feet, or the fact he was inspecting the precious memories displayed on her mantel with such curiosity that made her pause in nervous anticipation.

Was that really the same man she'd been butting heads with ten minutes earlier? And for months before that?

A traitorous little gasp gave away her presence and Nick's blue eyes met hers in the mirror above the mantel. He grinned and turned, giving her a view of his muscular chest, dusted with curling dark hair and decorated only by the KCPD badge and silver chain that hung around his neck. An appropriate zinger about winter temps and bare skin and common sense refused to form on her lips.

Must be the concussion that let a half-dressed man she had no interest in whatsoever warm her blood and cloud her thoughts.

"I went ahead and made myself at home." When Annie didn't speak, Nick took the initiative. He pointed to the sodden sweater and white T-shirt and socks draped over the radiator beside his charcoal-colored scarf. "I set the towels underneath so they won't drip on the floor. Hope that's okay. I checked the flue, too. I could start a fire for you if you have any wood."

"I don't." *Snappy conversationalist, Hermann.* She tried for something a little less reactionary. "Reitz and G.B. don't like the fire."

"Reitz and G.B.?"

"The cats."

He nodded toward the bundle of plaid flannel in her arms. "Is that for me?"

Oh, right. Stop staring. This was Nick Fensom— arch nemesis, pain in the posterior, overprotective bodyguard with a debt he thought he had to pay— not some hottie who could invade her personal space and turn her logic-loving brain to mush.

Shaking off the foggy stupor, Annie met him halfway across the living room and handed him the shirt. "I kept some of my parents' things after they passed away. My dad wasn't very tall either, but he was built like a tank. I wear it for a robe sometimes. It hangs off me like a sack, so I hope it's big enough to fit."

"It'll do."

The soft material strained to accommodate Nick's upper arms, but he managed to button it across his chest and roll up the sleeves. Annie wasn't sure if that tight fit was any less distracting than the bare skin had been, but at least the familiar brass-and-blue enamel badge he pulled from inside the collar reminded her of that coworker status they were supposed to share.

"Thanks." He took another few seconds to tuck the shirt into the waist of his jeans, and adjust the gun holstered at his hip. "You look refreshed."

"Are you kidding? I look like a New Year's Eve hangover, complete with tired eyes and pale skin." She tilted her eyes in the direction of the bandage and bump on her forehead. "Except for the colorful bruise, of course."

"I still vote for pretty."

"You said *refreshed*."

His gaze swept over her from her curling toes up to the damp curls of her hair, lingering for several timeless seconds at her lips, leading her to suspect that neither *pretty* nor *refreshed* was the adjective he'd really been thinking. Was he remembering that kiss at the hospital? Because suddenly, she couldn't think of anything besides the feel of Nick's hands tangled in her hair, and his mouth sliding over hers. Beneath the baggy fit of her sweats, Annie's body tightened in remembered awareness of his heat and hardness pressed against her body. He might as well have started a fire in the fireplace. Even now, his leisurely perusal turned her blood to molten honey, making her breasts feel heavy and her skin sensitive to even the soft brush of the cotton fleece she wore.

She must have taken a hard knock to the head. They were locked away from the rest of the world, cocooned by the snow and night outside. Just the two of them. And she wanted Nick Fensom to kiss her again. Desperately.

He broke the lingering silence. "I promised the cat I wouldn't argue with you anymore this evening."

"You promised the cat?" Desire short-circuited her brain, making sensible conversation impossible for the moment. The twitch of a tail at Nick's feet thankfully drew her attention to the Siamese twisting between his legs and stretching out across his feet. She clapped her hands. "Reitzie, shoo."

"He's all right. He was keeping my toes warm. You said you had *cats,* plural? I've seen only the one."

Move someplace. Do something. Her thoughts and emotions would get her into trouble otherwise. Annie scooted the big Siamese to his favorite chair and turned into the kitchen to start a pot of coffee. "That's Reitz. He's the extrovert. G.B. won't show himself until he decides he likes you."

"G.B.?"

"George Brett." The Kansas City baseball legend her dad had worshipped and her mom had crushed on.

"You named your cats after third basemen?"

Annie carried the coffeepot to the sink and filled it with water. "You know your sports history. My dad and I were both big fans of Missouri baseball—the St. Louis Cardinals and the Kansas City Royals. The '85 World Series tore him up—he didn't know who to root for. I had to be fair and represent both teams."

"That explains these pictures." Annie looked over the peninsula counter and stools at the end of the kitchen to see Nick pick up the last photograph she'd taken with her parents. "That one's old Busch Stadium and this is Kaufmann Park here in Kansas City before the big renovation. Is this your dad in the ball cap?"

Remembering that last, wonderful birthday together squeezed Annie's heart with fondness and sorrow. "Yes." She started the coffeemaker and went back to the living room. At least she had those memories to cling to. Nick set the frame back on the mantel and Annie reached up beside him to gently touch the image of the stocky man, dark-haired woman and happy teenager smiling back at her. "He and Mom took me to a Royals game for my seventeenth birthday."

The coffeemaker hissed and bubbled and filled

up the room with its rich, homey scent as Nick moved along the mantel, asking about each picture. The trip to Mount Rushmore, one to Washington, D.C. Holiday pictures, a school band competition. The self-indulgence of sharing memories and comparing childhood stories was a balm to Annie's lonesome soul, and as special a gift as anything she'd received since Adam had left. That Nick Fensom seemed so genuinely interested in her family history surprised her as much as her reaction to finding him half-dressed in her living room had.

"What's the scoop about this one here at the Baseball Hall of Fame?" He picked up the most recent photograph, taken a year and a half earlier at Cooperstown, New York. It featured her and a tall blob of Hall of Fame wrapping paper she'd matted behind the image of her standing in front of Stan Musial's statue. Nick traced the outline where she had cut out a part of her life from the picture. "Let me guess. Your friend here was wearing a rival Cubs jersey?"

If only. "Dad always wanted to go to Cooperstown, but never got the chance to. So my ex-fiancé and I made the trip summer before last in Dad's honor."

"Ex?"

"Musial was Dad's favorite player."

Grinning, Nick placed the photo back on the mantel. "And she carefully sidesteps *that* conversation."

"What's to say? Adam and I had different plans

for our lives, and he didn't think I would fit into his. Too much pink and paisley and obsession with my work, I guess."

"And not enough into his?" The grin flatlined. "I'm sorry. His loss."

Annie tilted her gaze to Nick's. From everything she'd heard through the grapevine, Adam had done just fine moving on with his life. "How do you mean?"

"Duh." Mischief danced across Nick's square features again. "You know more about Missouri baseball history than any woman I've met. What man in his right mind would give that up?"

Her grateful smile lasted until they reached the last picture of a Christmas tree, all lit up and full of presents, standing in front of her apartment windows.

"The walls are a different color," Nick observed. "But I recognize the woodwork around the windows. Looks like this apartment has been around awhile. You grew up here?"

Annie nodded. "It's where we were living when my parents died. And because I'd just graduated high school, I wasn't in any position to be buying a new place. I've remodeled the kitchen, repainted and added the cats, but it's pretty much the same."

The material around the buttons of Nick's borrowed shirt puckered as his chest expanded with a deep, measured breath. "You lost them both? So young?"

"Car accident." For a moment, the only sound in the place was the hissing and popping of the radiator coming on.

Automatically, she hugged her arms around her middle, reliving that horrible day when her principal and school counselor had pulled her out of physics class to give her the news about the jackknifed semi and pileup on the Interstate. She'd spent the rest of the week learning how to make funeral arrangements and read legal documents. There were no grandparents, no aunts or uncles—just some awesome school friends and the counselor—and a very empty apartment and future waiting for her night after night.

"You don't have any brothers and sisters? Any aunts or uncles?"

She shrugged. "Just little ol' me. The only child of two only children." She summoned her standard joke for when strangers questioned her family tree—or lack thereof. "Saves a lot of hassle shopping for Christmas presents."

Nick didn't laugh.

"Annie…"

She saw him reaching for her and knew she couldn't bear to be touched right now, not if she had any hope of holding on to the friendly civility of this conversation before bursting into tears. When his fingertips brushed against her sleeve, Annie pulled away and retreated to the kitchen. "Smells like the coffee's ready."

He followed right behind her. "Wait. You can't drop a bombshell like that and just walk away. You were only seventeen?"

The warm, fuzzy camaraderie was evaporating as the reality of her life in the present set in. She knew she was different from most people. She was cautious about what she revealed, preferred the black-and-white clarity of science and logic over emotional risks. She struggled with trust issues, interpersonal communication skills, the works. She'd been called everything from reclusive to odd to absentminded. And tonight she'd chosen to open up her personal life to *this* man of all people?

Suddenly, she was very busy pulling mugs out of a cabinet and unloading items from the fridge. "Do you take it black? Milk? Sugar? I've got leftover roast beef, or I can make a grilled cheese sandwich."

"Stop." Nick took the milk and set it on the counter. He scooted the mugs aside and plucked the loaf of bread from her hand when she reached for it, and turned her to face him. She stared straight at the badge hanging at the center of his chest, knowing what eye contact would do to the tears brimming in her eyes.

"Don't," she pleaded when she felt the tug on her wrists.

"Gonna do it anyway." He gathered her in his arms, turning her cheek into his shoulder, carefully avoiding the bandage and bruising on her forehead. "I'm so sorry about your folks."

"It happened ten years ago."

He tunneled his fingers beneath the hair at her nape and gently massaged her there. "Yeah, but I can tell you still miss them—probably more over the holidays than any other time of year. I shouldn't have said anything. Not tonight."

The holidays *were* the worst. And Nick got that? Mr. Insensitive, bull-in-the-china-shop of her world, understood what she was feeling? She must be so tired and beat-up after their long day that nothing was making any sense. Most of the time, she could handle the emptiness—she could live her life and function like a normal person. But talking about her past had stirred up too many memories for her to manage much of anything right now.

With a weary sigh, Annie relaxed her stiff posture. Her hands followed the path of Nick's belt around to the back of his waist to hold on to the comfort he offered. "You're a detective." She sniffled against the pillow of his shoulder, making one last, valiant effort at normalcy between them. "It's your nature to be nosy and ask questions."

But he didn't take the bait. A few tears spilled over and Nick's arms tightened, settling her more snugly against his chest. "Ah, slugger, I had no idea. I've got family coming out my ears and making me crazy sometimes, but I can't imagine losing a single one of them."

The flannel was soft against her cheek—the man beneath, solid and warm and caring. Annie closed her eyes and let the grief and fatigue and utter isolation burn through her eyelashes and spill over her cheeks. All the while, he whispered soft, wordless nothings against her ear, and his fingers stroked the back of her neck, soothing her. His warmth seeped into her chilled skin. His strength held her up for a few moments until it sank into her bones and tapped into her own reserves. Her tears dried up sooner than she expected, leaving her feeling far less melancholy than she'd been moments earlier. Her eyes felt gritty and her throat was parched, but she felt she could stand on her own two feet again and think straight. But for some reason, her hands couldn't seem to unlock the grip they held on the back of Nick's shirt. Some of her hair caught in the stubble of his beard as she nestled beneath his chin. "I'm sorry."

"Don't apologize for feeling what you feel. It's been a hell of a day—a hell of an investigation. I understand *this* a whole lot better than the woman who has to have a reason for everything." Were those his lips grazing the crown of her hair? "You're not who I thought you were."

"I know. I'm such an odd duck." That had been Adam's teasing endearment for her.

"Um, no. I was thinking that all that complicated stuff is just on the surface—that you're a real, live girl underneath it all."

Annie smiled at the teasing chuckle that vibrated his chest against her ear. "So I should add Pinocchio to my list of nicknames? Or is it Pinocchiette?"

"Well, I don't think 'odd duck' is a phrase I've ever used. Sounds more like something Grandpa would say. Surely, you wouldn't describe yourself like that. Wait a minute." He pulled back to frame her face between his hands. "Did he call you that? The guy you cut out of the picture?" The gleam of amusement in his eyes darkened almost as soon as she lifted her gaze to his. Then he was pulling her back into the hug, squeezing her tighter than before. "Forget I asked. Shutting my mouth now."

"That'll be the day." But there was no answering laugh. This time, Annie loosened her grip and wedged some space between them. She didn't need to mention he was spot-on about her ex's less-than-flattering description of her. "You're not who I thought you were, either," she conceded. "You are so different from anyone who's ever been a part of my world. I never know quite what to expect from you."

He brushed a swath of stray curls off her forehead. "Is that good or bad?"

"I don't know yet."

"Fair enough."

That perpetual glimmer of amusement in his eyes never returned. Instead, something earthy and intent darkened them to a rich midnight blue. And then Nick was dipping his head, moving closer.

Annie pushed her hands up past his collar to capture his jaw. "You promised."

"Technically, I never did." Still, he hesitated. "If you don't want this, say no."

A voice inside her, louder than the one in her head, urged her onto her toes to seal the kiss.

His lips covered hers in a gentle press of comfort, a warm breath of reassurance, a match to an inevitable flame.

Skimming her palms over the raspy stubble of his jaw, Annie slid her fingers into the thick, damp hair at his nape and opened her mouth beneath his. Her ready welcome sparked the feverish desire that had simmered under words and threats and misconceptions all day long—for days, weeks, months longer before that, no doubt, judging by the eager exploration of tongues and lips and the breathy moans between them.

Always a keen observer, Annie was suddenly overwhelmed by sensation after sensation. With every breath, her head filled with the rich scents of coffee and Nick's musky skin. Her fingers tugged at soft flannel to feel taut, warm skin underneath. She felt the ticklish abrasion of his beard against her throat, and the soothing caress of his lips and tongue following after.

Curiosity led her exploring hands across Nick's shoulders, down his sturdy arms, up into his hair. Need led them to the front of his shirt, where the buttons easily gave way to her determined fingers.

She tugged the soft cloth aside and branded her palms against hard curves of muscle and the tender spikes of his aroused male flesh. Nick's skin bunched and quivered beneath her grasping touch.

"Easy, slugger. Not so fast. There are two of us here." He seized her wrists and guided her arms back around his neck and walked his body into hers, driving her back against the countertop before reclaiming her mouth.

And just like that, the tables were turned. Every liberty she'd taken with Nick, his hands and mouth were doing to her. He slid his tongue along hers, twisting and tangling them together in soft, raspy caresses. He slipped his hands down to her butt and lifted her onto the counter, spreading her knees apart and moving between them, pressing the thick bulge of his zipper against the most sensitive part of her. Annie moaned against the sensual assault that robbed her of coherent thought and he dipped his moist, hot mouth to the hum in her throat. Her body, chilled the whole day long, was growing feverish from the inside out. The pores in her skin opened and she gasped for breath as the heat began to build. She squirmed atop the counter, bound by his hands and mouth and body, seeking some sort of release.

"Nick…I…please…"

Perhaps reading her thoughts more clearly than she, Nick slid his hands beneath her sweatshirt and found bare skin to claim. Her thighs clutched around his narrow hips. He palmed the lace of her bra and squeezed the achy nub of one breast. Annie tipped her head back, gasping at the shards of exquisite delight that shot through her like an electric current.

It had never been like this with her fiancé—this raw, this wild. With Adam there had always been steps, stages—seduction protocol. Making out with Adam had been a slow, planned process—methodical and predictable, which she thought had been perfect for her. Nick peeled away any pretensions of decorum and went straight to the want, to the need firing between them. His kiss was all instinct, all impulse, all passion. And she reveled in it.

"God, woman, I've never met anybody who gets into my head the way you do." He nuzzled his nose in her hair, his hard breaths and whispering lips teasing a sensitive bundle of nerves beside her ear. "You smell so good. You feel even better." He slipped his fingers beneath the elastic of her sweatpants and panties, pulling her to the edge of the counter, anchoring the weeping pressure between her thighs against the pulsing heat of his desire. The layers of cotton and denim between them couldn't hide what they both wanted. "You're all silk and fire and the biggest surprise of my life. Who knew, sitting across that meeting room table at KCPD all these months…so that's what the sparks were all about—"

"Stop talking, Nick."

This driving need was so far out of control, so far out of her realm of experience that Annie couldn't see the consequences. She couldn't see anything beyond the moment. She couldn't think. She only knew it felt good. It felt right. Coming to life in Nick's arms smashed any feelings of isolation. There was no past to mourn, no future to worry about. There was only now, only this, only Nick. She linked her heels behind his thighs, tunneled her fingers into the soft mess of his hair and pulled his mouth back to hers, seeking the force of his body moving against hers, assuaging her hunger for the powerful claim of his kiss.

"I just want to feel. I want to connect. I want—" An alarm bell went off inside her head. "What was that?"

"Connecting. Feeling. Magic." He kissed her with each word, pushed against her with every breath.

"Nick…" Annie tore her mouth from his with a breathless gasp. The ringing bell went off a second time, insisting that she regain a little common sense.

Nick pulled his hands to the neutral location of her waist. He pressed a chaste kiss to her swollen lips before easing some space between them. He rested his forehead against hers, his cobalt gaze looking down into her eyes. "It's your phone. Got an answering machine?"

"Of course." The machine on the far wall of the

kitchen rang again. Annie wondered at the stuttering rhythm of Nick's chest, heaving in and out like her own. Curiosity got her thinking again. And with thinking, a little bit of sanity returned. "But it could be the lab with the results from the serology tests I ran."

"Serology?" He pressed the gentlest of kisses against the bandage in her hairline.

"The study of body fluids like blood and..." He angled his head to kiss her lips, but Annie pushed him away before temptation overrode the reality of her life. "We need to stop. I'm sorry. I was tired and sad and I wasn't thinking. That was a—"

"Stopping," he interrupted sharply. He stepped back, holding his hands out to either side, breaking all contact except for the piercing intensity of those eyes. "But don't you dare say that was a mistake. It doesn't happen like that between two people if it's not supposed to. Didn't it feel right to you?"

"Of course it felt good. That's just hormones, Nick. It's a result of loneliness and guilt and fatigue. We needed the endorphins..." But the grim expression behind those beautiful eyes had no interest in the reasons why that kiss had happened. When the phone rang again, she seized the excuse to escape. She wasn't emotionally equipped to deal with the craziness Nick stirred up inside her right now. She hopped off the counter, landing on unsteady legs. "Let me get the phone."

"Damn if I can't think straight when you grab

on to me like that." If she didn't know better, she'd think she detected some kind of hurt shadowing his gaze as it followed her across the kitchen. But he looked away before she could even formulate a question, turning his attention to rebuttoning his shirt. "Maybe *you're* the one who needs to promise not to kiss *me*."

"Nick—"

Another ring. "Your phone? Blood tests? Serology?"

His sardonic tone was a reminder that *she* was the one who'd used work as an excuse to end that grope fest on the counter. Fine. Work. She could handle that a lot easier than trying to understand whatever Nick was feeling—or what she herself was feeling right now. After pulling her own clothes back into some semblance of order against the nerve endings still sparking across her skin, she picked up the phone. "Hello?"

There was a beat of silence before a raspy, barely audible voice answered. "Is this Annabelle Hermann?"

Annie. Odd duck. Pinocchio. Even *slugger.* Those nicknames were all fine. They made sense. But Annabelle? She'd only heard that name when she was in serious trouble from her parents or a teacher in grade school. Was this serious trouble?

"Annabelle?" the hoarse voice repeated. Definitely not the lab calling. Any friend or coworker would have identified himself. "It's you, isn't it?"

Oh, God. She knew that voice. From the alley.

"Who are you?" More silence. But the caller didn't hang up. She could hear him on the line, his slow, audible breathing crawling down her neck like the cold promise of winter. Or death. Oh, hell. Where had that image come from? She hugged her arm around her waist, feeling exposed, vulnerable—unsure of what was stalking her from the shadows. "I know you're there. What do you want? Hello?"

She saw a flash of movement from the corner of her eye a split second before Nick plucked the phone from her hand. "Who is this?" he demanded.

The click at the other end of the line was loud enough for her to hear. She turned to ask Nick if he thought she had reason to be spooked by the call, or if she was letting her off-kilter emotions create another error in judgment. But he'd already punched in the code to call back immediately to get the caller's number. She guessed that response was answer enough and wound both arms around her waist. She paced away from the wary tension radiating off Nick, but came right back when he muttered a curse and slammed the receiver back down on its cradle. "What is it?"

"No answer. No answering machine or voice mail, either." That left explanations like the caller turning off his phone, disposing of a prepaid cell, knowing it was her number calling back, but refusing to answer—any of which doubled her suspicion that the call was no accident. Nick immediately pulled his cell phone out of his pocket and punched in a number. Seeing him go into overprotective-cop mode again confirmed that she had every right to feel like someone was watching her, monitoring her location, maybe even intentionally trying to frighten her.

If that was the goal of that call, it was working.

"What did he say to you?" Nick demanded.

"Nothing. He just asked for me by name. He asked for Annabelle."

"Annabelle?" He shook his head. "I've never heard anybody call you that before. Is that how you're listed in the phone book?"

A sense of dreadful clarity fell like a weight through her body. "Yes."

"Hell."

"I think it was him. The man from the alley."

"And now he knows where you live." His call picked up at the other end of the line and he turned away. "Spencer? It's Nick."

Needing room to tamp down her frayed emotions and make some rational decisions, she left Nick and the small space of the kitchen, still so full of the memories of their ill-timed passion and the charged energy that was Nick himself. Annie scooped Reitz up off his favorite chair and plopped down in his place, stroking his ears and hugging his familiar warmth to her chest. If she needed any more evidence that her ordered world had tilted way out of balance over the past twenty-four hours, G.B. popped out from beneath the couch and jumped up into her lap, seeking attention, too.

Stereo purring offered little comfort. "Every time I drop my guard around that man, I get hit with something else."

"You still at the precinct?" She watched Nick stride out of the kitchen, checking the locks on her front door again. "Somebody's looking for Annie. I've got a phone number I need you to run for me. I'll wait." He walked past her to peek through the blinds at the front windows and check the locks there. "Are you saying I'm bad luck?"

He'd heard that comment? Fine. She wanted to discuss this burgeoning relationship that shouldn't be happening in the first place, anyway. "I'm saying you need to leave me alone. You need to leave, period. I have to focus on my work. I can't keep making mistakes."

"That phone call was intentional." He buzzed by her chair, phone still at his ear, and headed down the hallway. "Not some mistake."

"I'm talking about what happened in the kitchen. I'm talking about..." *Feelings.* Oh, damn. That could not be what was happening here. She was exhausted. The holidays made her feel blue. She had this stupid bump on the head that muddled her thoughts. Any one of those offered a plausible reason to explain why she'd dropped her guard and exposed every vulnerable nerve she possessed to this man. She supposed she could rationalize the physical attraction to those broad shoulders and blue eyes, but her discovery of his compassion and sense of humor, his die-hard loyalty to an idea, the heavy weight of the conscience he carried with him—she shouldn't notice or admire or care about any of those things. She shouldn't think Nick Fensom was the answer to any of her problems.

"Nick, wait." Annie dumped the cats off her lap and hurried down the hallway after him. "We need to remember that we have to work together. There's a serial rapist out there we're trying to identify. And now there's an accomplice, too? There couldn't be a worse time for us to…get involved."

"Involved?" She met him coming out of the bathroom, where she guessed he'd inspected the security of the window in there, too. "Who says we're involved?"

"Well, I don't go around practically having sex on the kitchen counter with just anyone." She'd never done anything so spontaneous and foolish and out of her comfort zone with any man, not even her fiancé. "I've never…I mean, I have, but never like…" She snapped her mouth shut, too embarrassed to elaborate on the boring parameters of her previous relationships.

He paused for a moment, granting her one sliver of truth. "Okay. So maybe things have gotten a little complicated between us tonight."

She jumped on the concession. "Exactly. I'd like

to go back to the way things were between us yesterday. There was friction, yes, but there was a pattern to our behavior. We accomplished—"

"Yeah, I'm still here," he muttered into the phone, gathering information from his partner and moving down the hallway again.

She tried to block his way into her bedroom, but Nick simply moved her aside and went straight to the window there. Locked. Everything was locked. She was perfectly safe. Right? Yet he still didn't relax the grim expression on his mouth or show any willingness to listen to reason.

He picked up a pen and pink notepad from the table beside her bed and jotted something down. "Yeah, Spence. Got it. Send somebody to check it out, will ya? I know he's probably long gone, but do it anyway. Thanks, buddy." He disconnected the call and tore off the top sheet of paper, holding up the phone number and an address she recognized. "That call came from a pay phone down by the Fairy Tale Bridal Shop."

That information shifted her attention. "Where Rachel Dunbar was killed?"

"Same neighborhood. Spencer is going to send a squad car around to see if anybody's in the area. But I'm guessing that crackpot's long gone."

She definitely needed to think like a criminologist and not a woman fighting her feelings for the wrong guy right now. With a nod of renewed determination, Annie opened her closet and pulled out a fresh pair of blue jeans. "You have to drive me down there so I can dust for prints and look for any kind of trace he may have left behind. And because we're right there, I can get my car and drive myself home."

"No."

She tossed the jeans onto her bed and went to her dresser to pull out some knee socks. "Time is a factor, Nick. If that guy left any evidence, I need to find it sooner rather than later."

"No, you are not driving your car or coming back here by yourself."

Her shoulders sagged with a groan of frustration. They lifted just as quickly as she crossed the room to push him out into the hall. But as soon as Nick braced his feet, he became an immovable object stuck in her bedroom doorway. "What are you doing?"

"I need to get some warm clothes on if we're going uptown to that pay phone." She pushed at the center of his chest, but the remembered sensations of strength and heat only made her back away. "Your things on the radiator are probably dry by now."

"I never said—"

"I need to dust that phone for prints. If there's any chance that guy took off his gloves, we might be able to ID him. Maybe he left a shoe print in the snow—with temperatures dropping and the snow and slush freezing over, I could make a casting. I can at least take a photograph."

"If you aren't the stubbornnest…" He nodded, and suddenly, that handsome grin was back in place. "All right. Let's bundle up and get out of here."

"Why don't I just drive my car back afterward and you can go home and get some sleep?"

The grin vanished as quickly as it had appeared. "Twenty-four hours ago, a man nearly killed you to get his hands on the evidence in your possession. He knows where you live. Are you going to trust that he thinks he got everything and has no reason to come back to finish what he started?"

"If you stay here, we can't…you have to promise—"

"You'll know when I make a promise to you, Annie." Before she could guess his intent, his hand snaked out to cup the back of her neck. His fingers tunneled into the curls there and her skin dotted with goose bumps, remembering his touch. He stroked his thumb against the thumping beat of her pulse. "I am keeping you safe whether you like it or not. You're right. We are on this task force job together—so you do your brainy thing and I'll do what I do so that you can get us whatever clues you can. I'm tired of this Rose Red bastard and his sick fan club having the upper hand on us. This investigation will not be compromised. You will not be hurt. Not while there's breath in my body. Understood?"

Annie nodded, reading the promise in those dark blue eyes. She reached up to wind her fingers around his wrist, holding on to his coiled strength, finally resigning herself to his round-the-clock protection.

The tone of his voice gentled, but the vow behind it was no less adamant. "It may be coincidence that there was some jackass in a big car who doesn't know how to drive in this weather or thought it'd be a nice practical joke to drench us in snow and ice. Maybe that call came from a phone a block from where Rachel Dunbar died because there are no other pay phones in the city. But that attack this morning was no mistake. I don't buy two coincidences, much less three. Now, either I get the couch or I'm sleeping out there on the landing. And I don't think the neighborhood-watch guy is going to like that."

"I've got blankets and pillows for the couch." Annie pulled away and picked up the clothes off her bed. There were no more arguments to be made. She resigned herself to having Nick's company 24-7, so she'd better shore up the resolve that guarded her heart before she foolishly forgot that they weren't *involved*. "I'll get changed and grab my kit."

Chapter Seven

Annie climbed out of Nick's silver Jeep and squinted against the bright morning sun reflecting off the blanket of snow that sloped up to his parents' front porch. Her headache and occasional wooziness from standing or turning too quickly seemed to have gone after a good night's sleep. But her trepidation about visiting the two-story yellow-and-white Victorian—and all the people she'd met at the hospital gathered there—made her cling to the door handle and consider climbing back inside.

"This will be a quick stop." Nick's door shut behind her and she transferred her grip to the strap of her purse hanging across her chest. He circled around the car and joined her on the curb. "I just need to pick up a few things. I'll get my bag and clothes and we'll be gone."

The big house and sprawling yard certainly looked big enough to accommodate all of them. But still, Nick had to be twenty-eight? Twenty-nine? "You live with your mom and dad?"

"Very funny. Natalie and I have our own apartments in town. But because Noah, Nadine and Nate are home from college, and Grandma and Grandpa Fensom are visiting, Nat and I came home for the holidays to make it a real family reunion." He touched his hand to the small of her back to guide her through the snow at the curb onto the cleared sidewalk. "That way, if we get caught up in a twenty-four-hour game of Risk, or want to watch the complete *Lord of the Rings* DVD marathon, we don't have to worry about cutting out on the fun early, or showing up late for breakfast. Besides, the midnight snacks here are way better than anything I've got at my place."

She moved away from the brush of his hand, more alarmed by the instant tingling of heat and awareness she felt than by the holiday traditions he described. "You played a game for twenty-four hours?"

Even in this well-tended, tree-lined suburban neighborhood, Nick kept looking back and forth, scanning up and down the street, taking note of cars driving past and neighbors shoveling or snow-blowing their driveways and walks. "I won, by the way. Reclaimed the title that Nate stole from me last year."

Despite the friendly chatter and clear sunshine, he didn't seem any more relaxed about watching over her than he'd been last night. But if he could pretend he hadn't moved closer to shield her from a direct line of sight from the street, then she could pretend her nerves weren't perched on a thin ledge, waiting to jump at anything that moved in the shadows. "With your competitive streak? Who could believe that?"

He laughed at her sarcasm, pausing for her to precede him up the painted white steps onto the porch. "Did you and your folks ever do anything crazy like that for the holidays?"

Annie's boots stuttered to a halt. He was bringing up her parents? After the horrific loss she'd shared with him last night? But then she looked up into her reflection in his wraparound sunglasses and saw the sadness and shock there. A pang of guilt made her look away. Steve and Amaryllis Hermann had been supportive, fun-loving parents. She was doing them a disservice by focusing on the loss instead of remembering the good times, too.

She looked up again and watched her face transform into a wistful smile. "On New Year's Day, we used to set up all the TVs we had in the apartment in the living room, so Dad could watch as many football games as he could. Mom and I would set up a card table and put together jigsaw puzzles or play cards. The only rule we had was to have fun and not work. We'd order pizza or pop popcorn for dinner. Sometimes we'd stay in our pajamas all day."

Nick's answering smile felt like some kind of reward she'd earned for sharing that part of herself. Her parents were probably smiling, too. "All play and no work. Sounds like a celebration I could get into."

That he made the effort to include memories of her family amid all the talk of his own warmed a chilly place inside Annie, and fortified her for what promised to be another challenging social situation for her. He pulled open the storm door and knocked on the welcoming red door inside. "Hello? Anybody home?"

"Do-o-or," someone yelled. A herd of trampling feet stormed the door from the opposite side.

Annie couldn't stop herself from startling when the door swung open with a flourish. But the hand at her back reminded her there was no retreat.

"Nicky!" Trudy Fensom threw her arms wide and welcomed her eldest son with a hug and a kiss.

"Hey, Mom. Grandma." Nick moved on to his white-haired grandmother for another hug and kiss. As he moved through the crowd, there were handshakes with his father and grandfather, a pinch on the cheek for one of his sisters and a smack on the shoulder for his youngest brother.

Annie thought she could slip inside the door and wait for all the greetings to finish. But Nick's mom pulled her into a hug. "Welcome, Annie."

"Hi, oh." She felt honor-bound to hug her back. "Thanks."

She was reintroduced to his grandmother, Connie, who squeezed her hands and smiled. "You're looking much better this morning, dear. There's a rosy glow to your cheeks." She reached up and patted Annie's face. "Oh, but you're cold. We'd better get something warm inside you."

"I'm fine, thank you."

But Connie tugged on her daughter-in-law's sleeve and the two hurried off to the kitchen. Then she was ushered through the same lineup of handshakes and hi's Nick had passed through. Clay Fensom took her coat. Noah, no, this one was Nate, scarcely more than a teenager, blushed.

"I'm Nicolas, remember?" Nick's grandfather took Annie's hand and slipped it through the crook of his arm to lead her along the hallway next to the stairs. "We're just getting ready to sit down for some breakfast. Have you eaten yet?"

As charmed as she was by the gallant escort, she was already starting to feel the clan closing in on her. "Thank you, but we can't stay long. We have to get down to the precinct. There's a task force briefing this morning."

"We'll wrap up something for you, then." He took her through a squared-off archway into a spacious kitchen with tall white cabinets and green tile backsplash. "Connie, we need to get some meat on this girl's bones. What can we send with her?"

Trudy pulled a cookie sheet of scones from the oven and swatted Nick's hand away from the steaming treats before pointing to the long farm table already set for breakfast. He snatched up a strip of crisp bacon and jostled aside the other brother—

Noah, a shade taller and skinnier than Nick—to get first pick from a basket of baked goods.

"Where's Nell?" he asked around bites.

"She went out to walk the dog," Noah answered. A dog was part of all this, too? "Nadine's in the shower, getting out of setting the table."

"I am not." A new voice entered the fray as Nadine Fensom walked in, wearing a black-and-gold Mizzou sweatshirt. "It was your turn to set the table. I've got dishes after we eat. Hi, Annie."

"Hi."

Nadine walked over to the table and pulled out a chair. Nick leaned down and pressed a kiss to the top of her head. "Morning, shortstuff."

This was beginning to look far too cozy, far too much like he was settling in for a big holiday meal while she floundered as the odd man out. He'd promised this would be a quick stop. Annie held up the watch on her wrist. "Nick, remember the time."

He poured himself a glass of milk and gave her a thumbs-up as he downed half of it.

"Here, dear." Grandpa Nicolas pulled out a stool at the island counter for her. "Will you at least join us for a cup of coffee? Nicky always has a glass of milk with breakfast."

When she realized he was politely waiting for her to sit before he did the same, Annie's *no, thank you* died on her lips and she replaced it with a smile instead. She was starting to get an idea of who had gotten the charm in this family. His bullying grandson might give her fits, but this one was hard to resist. She supposed one cup of coffee couldn't hurt, and climbed onto the stool. "Do you have any sugar?"

Seeming delighted that their guest had asked for something, Nick's father quickly pulled down a mug while Natalie brought her the coffee carafe, a spoon and the sugar bowl.

Annie was cradling the warm mug between her hands and inhaling the fragrant brew when Nick walked by with two more strips of bacon in his hand. He took a bite and chewed around his words. "Give me five minutes to pack all my gear. Then we can go."

"You're leaving me?" No. He was already gone. She heard his booted feet on the stairway as his grandmother set a platter of something warm and spicy on the counter in front of Annie. She was being bombarded with delicious smells and friendly conversation, and needed to concentrate on the rest of the busy family to keep up. She took a deep breath. She could manage five minutes on her own if she occupied herself with something to eat. "Cinnamon rolls?"

"Freshly made." Connie's smile was as warm and irresistible as her husband's.

Annie surrendered. Socializing like this was stressful for her because of that pesky shy gene and the fact it was so different from her day-to-day life. But it was good stress. It was safe stress.

Besides, the warm icing was oozing over the edge of the platter, tempting her to run her finger beneath the rim and pop the yummy sweetness into her mouth. "I love cinnamon rolls."

Truer to his word than Annie had given him credit for, Nick came back down the stairs five minutes later. Leaving seemed to require just as many hugs and side conversations. But Trudy's announcement that the food on the table would get cold had an instant hushing effect, and, just like that, Annie found herself back out on the front porch with Nick. He carried a duffel bag over his shoulder while she carried a plastic container filled with enough baked goodies to either make her fat or make her extremely popular at the task force meeting.

She opened the corner of the plastic tub one more time and inhaled the heavenly scents. "Your mom and grandmother are fabulous cooks. I don't know which one I liked better."

"I'd say the cinnamon rolls." He reached over and flicked a tiny glob of icing from her cheek.

Still enervated from the mad dash of family, the cold brush of leather across her skin had an oddly warming effect. She covered her cheek with her own glove and turned away, hoping a blush hadn't given away her reaction to the unexpected intimacy. She was the one who'd insisted on maintaining a professional distance from each other. It would be difficult to persuade him they were nothing more than amicable coworkers if she kept turning into a puddle of goo every time the man touched her.

She was facing down the street when a gray schnauzer wearing a red sweater came trotting down the sidewalk, dragging his leash behind him. "Nick, is that your dog?"

"Mozart?" He made a shrill whistle through his teeth. "Mozart!"

With a yapping bark, Mozart bounded up the stairs. He put his front paws up on Nick's thigh, wagging his stump of a tail in furious excitement. After a scratch around his ears, the dog dropped down onto all four paws to sniff his way over to Annie.

"Is he friendly?" His tail was still wagging as he climbed up Annie's pant leg. Apparently so.

The thump of Nick's bag hitting the porch startled the dog and he scooted behind Annie's legs. She didn't need to see Nick's face to read the tension straining those broad shoulders. She looked up and down the street with him. "Where's your sister?"

"I'll go find her." He handed her the dog's leash and headed down the steps. "It may be nothing. Maybe Mozart got away from her."

"But?" She could tell he didn't think this was *nothing*.

He turned and pointed a finger at her. "Stay put. I mean it this time. Keep the little noisemaker with you."

He was jogging down the front walk before she could answer.

"Stay put" meant stay on the porch, right? Not venture back inside and possibly alarm his family? Nick dashed down to the four-way stop and scanned every direction before deciding to turn right. Once he'd disappeared from sight around the last house, Annie set down the tub of rolls and scones and knelt to give Mozart the tummy rub he'd rolled over onto his back for. "So you're not a guard dog, huh?"

If she had to wait, had to stay put, then Annie fell back on what she did best. Mozart seemed happy to let her roll him from side to side and check him for any signs of injury. He was less thrilled when she tugged at his paws. If there'd been some kind of accident, the dog hadn't been a part of it. The sweater was clean except for a black smudge across the dog's shoulder blades, as though he'd scooted beneath something sooty or—she leaned down to give it a sniff—greasy.

Annie got a lick on the chin for getting too close and she quickly pulled away. Her training wanted her to analyze that smudge. But her kit was in Nick's car, and if this was a situation where she truly needed to get her kit, then she should be calling 9-1-1.

She was almost ready to alert the family when she caught a glimpse of a dark brown ponytail bobbing beyond the railing of the porch. Annie exhaled a sigh of relief as Nell trudged through the snow around the corner of the house, having cut through the neighbor's backyard.

Nell grabbed the stair railing with her bare hand and mounted the first two steps before she saw she had company. "Annie." The teenager dropped her gaze to the dog. "Oh, good. You caught Mozart."

"Hi, Nell." Annie was still in analysis mode when she stood. But she didn't need to be a scientist to see the puffy redness rimming those young blue eyes Nell tried to hide. Or to note the thick red welts circling the girl's exposed wrist. How hard did a dog have to yank on his leash to leave that mark? Annie glanced down at the tail-wagging fireball. This one wasn't big enough to do it. "Are you okay?"

Seeing the injury had caught Annie's eye, Nell tugged her coat sleeves down over her fingers. She climbed the last few steps onto the porch where she could turn and survey the neighborhood. "Where's Nick?"

"Out looking for you." The teen's eyes lighted everywhere except on Annie. Nothing suspicious about that. Much. "You didn't answer my question. How did you get hurt?"

Now the blue eyes blinked and looked straight at her. "That's not what you asked."

Annie quickly sorted through her first meeting with Nell Fensom, with the texting and secrecy and the 7th Street gangbanger Nick had mentioned. No wonder Nick had reacted with such concern. "Your walk with Mozart didn't, by any chance, include a rendezvous with your boyfriend, did it?"

Nell's slim shoulders tried to puff up like her brother's. "Maybe if my family didn't give me so much grief about Jordan, I wouldn't have to sneak out of the house to see him."

"Did he grab your wrist and hurt you?"

The teen's delicate shoulders sagged. "It was an accident. Mozart started chewing on the backseat of Jordan's car where we were parked and Jordan threw him out. I went to open the door to catch him before he ran off, but Jordan grabbed me and said we weren't done talking." She massaged her wrist, no doubt replaying the incident in her head. Her worried blue eyes sought out Annie's. "Don't tell Nick, okay?"

Annie's heart lodged in her chest. Nick's gut had been right about this guy. "If your boyfriend hurt you, I can't keep that a secret. I'm a mandated reporter."

"Fine. Then nothing happened." She snatched the dog's leash from Annie's hand and headed for the door.

"Nell—"

The teenager hesitated before pulling open the storm door. "Jordan asked me about Nick."

"What did he want to know?"

"It wasn't like before, you know, like, 'Is your brother gonna get in my face for kissing you?'" She glanced over her shoulder and Annie could see that Nell's gut was telling her something was wrong with her relationship, too. "He wanted to know what kind of cop Nick was. He heard that Nick used to work on the anti-gang squad, and wanted to know if he still did."

"Is Jordan part of a gang?"

"He says he's not. And he doesn't hang with them at school, but…"

"But why ask about it?" Annie turned back to the street, searching for Nick. He needed to be hearing this, not her. She hadn't raised a kid, didn't have any little sister she'd practiced giving advice to. But she'd weathered a lot of hard stuff on her own. Nell was lucky to have a family who cared. "Sometimes the people who bug you the most are right. Even when you don't want them to be. If you think this Jordan is just using you—"

"But I love Jordan. And he loves me. He's always been so sweet. I don't understand why he got so mad."

"Here." Annie opened the flap of her purse and fished inside for her card wallet. She pulled out one of her business cards and handed it to Nell. "Call me sometime. Maybe we could meet for tea or a soda. Just the two of us. We could talk. I bet it's hard to get some quiet time to think when you're surrounded by so many outgoing people."

Nell took the card and summoned half a smile. "You noticed, huh?"

"It doesn't take a forensic scientist to figure that out."

The smile widened and she stuffed the card into

her coat pocket. "Thanks. We'll see." And then the smile vanished. "Jordan?"

Annie spun around to see an ice-blue Impala with a young Latino driver turn onto the street. With its music thumping loudly enough to vibrate the icicles hanging from the gutters, the car cruised by the front of the house at a snail's pace, giving Annie plenty of time to see the boy's olive-skinned face and dark eyes. He put two fingers to his lips and blew a kiss to Nell. A harmless enough gesture if Annie hadn't just heard about his temper and his curiosity about a former anti-gang cop.

"Come on." She reached for Nell's arm. Annie didn't like being this exposed to watching eyes, not after last night. And a chill crawled right up her spine when Jordan's dark gaze settled on her and he blew a second kiss. That wasn't flirting. That was cockiness. That was a taunt. It felt like a threat. Annie pulled the storm door open herself. "We'd better get inside."

"Nell?" The crunch of snow beneath Nick's boots announced his return as he followed Nell's trail through the side yard. "Thank God you're home. I circled around half the block looking for— Hey!"

As soon as Nick stepped into view, the two-fingered kiss turned sideways and Jordan mimicked the action of shooting a gun.

At Nick.

"Get inside!" Nick warned, reaching beneath his jacket and charging toward the street.

"Jordan!"

Annie shoved open the door, remembering Nick taking aim at the man who'd attacked her. But the Impala's big engine roared to life and Nell's boyfriend sped away. "Garza!"

Nick had pulled out his phone, not his gun. He ran out into the street, shouting to the number he'd dialed—traffic patrol, most likely—while Jordan Garza careened around the corner without stopping and raced out of sight.

Annie took in Nell's white-knuckled grip on the door frame and wondered which player in that thirty-second scenario had scared her more. When Nick turned around and cut a new path straight through the snow to get to his sister, Annie knew *her* answer. "Your brother would never hurt you. If your boyfriend is giving you ultimatums, think about that when you choose whose side you want to be on."

Nick came up the porch steps two at a time. "Call me when you find him. Fensom out." Nick disconnected the call and stuffed the phone into his pocket, never breaking stride as he pulled open the storm door and reached for his baby sister. "You okay?"

"You called the cops on Jordan?" Nell burst into tears and scooted inside with the dog, avoiding Nick's touch. The red door slammed and she charged straight up the stairs, past her parents and siblings who'd heard the shouts and the car and had come to check out the commotion.

Nick threw up his hands. "What did I do? Is she all right?"

"Nothing you can fix." Nick glanced at her sharply as if that possibility had never occurred to him.

He exchanged a puzzled look with his father, then closed the storm door and picked up his duffel bag. "She was talking to you, wasn't she? Are you going to explain this to me?"

"I'll try." Annie picked up the tub of sweet rolls and started down the stairs, but he quickly caught up and fell into step beside her.

"Am I going to like this explanation?"

"Probably not."

Chapter Eight

What had been a windy, gloppy, frozen mess for New Year's Day had settled into a business-as-usual January 2 outside Fourth Precinct headquarters. Road crews were already busy clearing the downtown streets and laying down cinders and salt. Uniformed and civilian personnel on KCPD's second watch schedule were hunched down inside their coats, catching up on holiday vacations and whining about the weather as they trudged along the sidewalk between tall evergreens whose dark green branches hung low with snow. In addition, several cars and news vans were parked along the curb, hinting that word had leaked out about the Rose Red Rapist's latest attack. This morning had all the makings of a normal day at work.

But there had been nothing *normal* about this day thus far. Not the early morning social hour at the Fensom house, not the troubling heart-to-heart she'd had with Nell Fensom, and certainly not the conversation she'd shared on the ride to work. In scarcely more than twenty-four hours, she'd learned that Nick Fensom could be annoying, bossy, stubborn, protective, sexy, impulsive, caring and maybe even a little funny. But she'd never have pegged him for the moody, surly man who followed her out the front entrance of the KCPD parking garage.

"Let's keep moving." Apparently, if he couldn't keep his youngest sister safe from a dubious boyfriend, then he intended to double his efforts to protect Annie.

Annie startled at the touch of Nick's hand on her arm. But she quickly pulled away and hurried over the crosswalk before the steadying strength and distracting heat of even that impersonal contact filled her head with images from last night that were alternately comforting and erotic and oh, so out of place from anything that felt familiar in her day-to-day world.

With Nick following closely on her heels, she turned into the cold north wind and followed the sidewalk up to the gray granite steps leading to the building's double-glass doors. But not even the sharp air that bit through the layers of wool and cotton she wore could dull the vivid memory of Nick's kiss, or fool her into thinking he'd gotten over his guilt trip and would give up his pledge to be her shadow anytime soon.

Their late-night visit to the abandoned pay phone had been full of strained silences and terse exchanges. And while she'd taken photos of several different footprints, the phone itself was not only free of fingerprints, but it had also been wiped clean, leaving her without so much as a skin cell to process. Frustration and exhaustion had left her eager to go home and climb into the comfort of her own bed. But once Annie slipped beneath her quilts, she'd lain awake, hypernaturally aware of every sound and movement coming from the other side of her closed bedroom door.

Other than a couple of sleepovers with her ex-fiancé, Adam, she'd lived alone for ten years. Last night she'd had a man, wearing a pair of jeans and nothing more, making himself at home out in her living room. It had been distracting to hear how Nick had tossed and grumbled, trying to find a comfortable position on the sofa. Finally, he'd gone to the kitchen for a glass of milk. Upon his return, she'd smiled when she heard him arguing softly with Reitz over who had claim to the pillows.

But it had been even more unsettling a few minutes later to hear his quiet steps coming down the hallway, stopping outside her bedroom door. She'd closed her eyes and feigned sleep when he silently nudged the door open and stood there, watching over her in the darkness, finally deciding that she was safe enough for him to relax his vigil and get a few hours of shut-eye himself.

This morning, she'd dared to hope that things would return to normal between them. Trade a few quips. Push each other's buttons. Work together amicably enough while maintaining a professional distance. No kissing, no touching, no illusions that she might actually have feelings for the man. But the incident with Jordan Garza this morning had put the kibosh on that.

Well, at least Nick hadn't kissed her.

"Hold up," Nick warned, catching her arm and holding on this time as they reached the double front doors. He peeled off his sunglasses and peered through the glass into the building's lobby. "Looks like there's a crowd in there."

Annie's breath steamed through her nose. She tugged against his grip, sensing his retreat away from the promise of warmth and a familiar work routine inside the building. "It's a press conference. Looks like Dr. Kilpatrick cut short her holiday vacation with Sheriff Harrison. She must be briefing them on Rachel Dunbar's murder."

Cameras and sound equipment, power cords and spotlights wove through a crowd of twenty or so reporters and their crews. The coolly elegant blonde at the podium pressed her lips together, ending her statement, and a dozen hands shot up. The microphones and cameras drifted forward, then retreated, like the ebb and flow of a human tide as forensic psychologist and fellow task force member Kate Kilpatrick called on one man in the crowd.

Annie took note of a couple of uniformed officers positioned around the lobby, but even their eyes were focused on the woman in the spotlight. The only person not hanging on every word was the tall, uniformed sheriff in a cowboy hat, standing just behind Dr. Kilpatrick. He was watching everyone else in the lobby, his sharp eyes and protective stance needlessly reminding Annie just how dangerous their hunt for the Rose Red Rapist could be. Only a few months earlier a stalker masquerading as the rapist had terrorized Dr. Kilpatrick, a well-spoken woman who also served as the task force's press liaison.

Boone Harrison, a small-town sheriff who'd originally come to Kansas City to investigate his sister's murder, had interfered with the task force's investigation. But he'd wound up being in the right place at the right time to save Dr. Kilpatrick's life. Although they played down the attraction between them, the sheriff had also become a fixture in Dr. Kilpatrick's personal life—and judging by his watchful stance, he believed there was still something dangerous out there she needed protection from.

Were Nick's instincts right, too? Was there something dangerous out there after Annie, as well?

A chill that wasn't entirely due to the bitter wind raised goose bumps across her skin, indicating there might be more bravado than bravery to Annie's courage. But she pulled her chin from inside the collar of her coat and reached for the door handle anyway.

"You okay?" Nick's fingers squeezed her hand and she shivered outright.

"I don't do really well with big crowds of people."

"If you can survive my family, you can survive this." At last, a glimpse of the Nick she knew. "Let's just get upstairs to the conference room."

"Right."

She opened the door and they were greeted by a blast of heat and noise as Kate Kilpatrick finished her answer and the reporters' hands shot into the air again. Every camera was flashing. Every voice clamored to be heard.

Dr. Kilpatrick pointed to the female reporter with the long dark hair, standing at the front of the group beside a news cameraman. "Ms. Owen?"

The camera's light brightened, filming Dr. Kilpatrick's response to the reporter's question. "Do you believe the Rose Red Rapist's crimes have escalated to murder? How do you intend to proceed with the investigation without any witness to interrogate?"

"There's more than eyewitness testimony involved when it comes to solving a crime." Kate's evenly modulated voice never wavered, despite the taunt coloring the reporter's tone. "We look at victimology, suspect profiling, forensic evidence—"

"But there is no forensic evidence from Ms. Dunbar's murder," the reporter interrupted. "According to my sources, at any rate. Can you confirm the disappearance of that evidence? That it's no longer in KCPD's hands?"

"I'm not sure where your source would have gotten that information."

"Are you saying there *is* evidence?" the reporter prodded. "What did you find?"

Sheriff Harrison grumbled something and moved up behind Dr. Kilpatrick. But she raised a hand, warning him back to his place without ever taking her eyes off the female reporter. "I can neither confirm nor deny that report at this time. However, our investigation continues to move forward."

"The people of Kansas City will be glad to hear that." But there was little praise in the woman's aggressive tone. "My source also says there was a second attack at the scene of Rachel Dunbar's murder. Is there evidence from that crime? Can it identify the rapist?"

An undercurrent of softly voiced comments and sidebar conversations increased the noise bouncing off the lobby's stone walls.

"There was another attack?"

"Who did he hurt?"

"Do you have a name?"

Dr. Kilpatrick leaned into the microphone on the podium and tried to defuse the tension building in the room. "We don't believe the Rose Red Rapist is responsible for the second attack."

"But the two crimes are related, right?"

All the questions and comments got lost in the shock buzzing in Annie's ears. They were talking about *her*. Her voice tightened to a whisper. "How does that woman know I lost the evidence?"

"She doesn't." Nick bumped into Annie's back when she stopped and she stumbled forward. But his hands quickly folded around her shoulders, steadying her, pulling her half a step closer to whisper against her ear. "And you didn't lose it. It was taken. Forcibly. That reporter's fishing for information."

Annie watched the reporters' curiosity morph into excitement, even panic, as they got wind of the new twist in KCPD's investigation. "What source is she talking about? Do you think it was that man who called my apartment last night?"

With his hands still on her shoulders, Nick nudged her forward again. "Let Dr. Kilpatrick handle it. I've got a bad feeling about this. There are too many people on edge in here." He shifted his hold and wrapped his hand around Annie's, moving in front of her to pull her along more quickly. "The stairs are closer. We'll take those up to the second floor and catch the elevator there."

"You and your gut." Annie hurried her short legs to keep up with his. "You know, your internal viscera scares me more than the shadows moving through that alley did."

"If my internal viscera had been working last night, none of this…" Nick's gaze darted over the top of Annie's head and he cursed. "Too late."

"Too late for what?"

He tapped her cheek, pushing her gaze toward the reporters to see what he'd seen, even as he tightened his grip on her hand and pulled her past the open stairs. "They can follow us there. We need a closed door between us."

For a split second, Annie's feet refused to work. One of the television cameramen had pulled his eye away from his screen to watch the man and woman skirting around the edge of the lobby. Without taking his eyes off Annie, he tapped the shoulder of the dark-haired woman with a microphone standing next to him. "You think that's her?" he asked the reporter. "She looks beat up."

"Annie. Move." Nick nearly pulled her off her feet.

Her pulse raced into overtime, fueling her panic and pouring adrenaline into her steps.

The cadre of reporters turned as one, taking note of the couple scurrying to the elevators. Like a shifting flock of birds, all eyes and lights and camera lenses turned their attention toward them.

"Is she another victim?"

"He's one of those task force cops," another one confirmed. "I interviewed him for the paper."

"What about her? She's been hurt. Who is she?"

Nick punched the elevator's call button half a dozen times. "Come on."

Annie squeezed Nick's free hand between both of hers as the flock changed course and pursued them across the lobby.

"Annabelle Hermann?"

The memory of a man's breathy voice chilled the blood in her veins and she turned. Did she know that voice? "Who said that?"

She tried to search the approaching crowd, but they were shifting equipment, jostling for position—coming after her.

"CSI Hermann?" The click of high-heels hurried across the lobby, and the noise that followed drowned out any chance of identifying the source of that voice. "You *are* CSI Annabelle Hermann, right?"

"How did you know?" She wasn't wearing her vest or any other visible ID. Annie scanned the crowd of reporters and concerned citizens, wondering which man had sounded so ominously familiar. But there were so many faces. Too many.

The woman reporter's stunning, caramel-skinned beauty seemed menacing as she thrust her microphone toward Annie. "You're on the task force, dear. We know all your names."

Nick pulled her closer. "I knew it was a bad idea to list us in the paper."

Suddenly, the lobby was far too hot and way too crowded and Annie longed for the bitter cold and empty sidewalk outside. She trained her ears to the sound of gears locking into place and counterweights lowering the elevator down to the first floor. But that focused hearing also made the barrage of questions assaulting her crystal clear.

"I'm Vanessa Owen, evening news," the woman introduced herself, putting herself front and center among the gathering group. She snapped her fingers to the tall, dark-haired cameraman beside her. "Damien, are you getting this? Get a shot of her face."

He nodded. "Got it."

"Can you tell us what happened?" Vanessa asked. "Were you attacked by the Rose Red Rapist?"

"No." Annie tugged her stocking cap lower over her forehead and squinted into the light of the television camera. "There was no rose."

"Then how were you injured? That's a nasty bruise."

The natural instinct to answer a question put to her drew the words out of Annie's stunned thoughts. "I was at the crime scene. Early New Year's morning."

Nick pushed her behind him, putting his body between Annie and the thrust of the female reporter's microphone. "We're not here to answer questions."

The reporter ignored his defensive stance and leaned to one side to speak to Annie. "But you were attacked while investigating Rachel Dunbar's murder?"

"Yes."

A dozen lights flashed and Annie had to close her eyes.

Clutching the back of Nick's jacket, she felt,

rather than saw, him take a deep breath to form a more imposing barrier. "We're done here."

"Excuse me, Detective." Vanessa must have turned her attention to Nick. "The women of Kansas City are afraid. Don't you think we have the right to know about what's lurking in the shadows? If members of the police department are now falling victim to this madman—"

Annie opened her eyes and whispered into the leather of Nick's jacket, "I'm not another victim."

"—then how can the rest of us possibly feel safe?"

Right now, Annie needed Nick to stand against the onslaught, but she found strength of her own to make herself heard. "I wasn't assaulted by the Rose Red Rapist. There's no evidence of that. Don't put that lie out there or people will panic."

"Can you tell us who attacked you? Who killed Ms. Dunbar?" Vanessa nodded to her cameraman. "Damien?"

Her tall, dark-haired assistant had swung around to one side, capturing an image of Annie pressed against the elevator doors. "I've still got her, Van. We're rolling."

Apparently he'd crossed some unmarked line and gotten too close because Nick put his hand on the camera lens, giving it a little shove as he pointed it down to the floor. "Back off, *Damien*."

Damien clutched the camera to his stomach, fury coloring his neck as he squared off against Nick.

"I've got rights. This is an expensive piece of equipment. I'm doing my job."

"So am I."

"Vanessa." Kate Kilpatrick's firm voice came through the loud speakers, cutting sharply across the room, interrupting the standoff and momentarily silencing the reporters. "*I* speak for the task force. You'll direct your questions to me or I'll have you and your cameraman banned from HQ. Detective Fensom and CSI Hermann have work to do. They are not your concern."

Annie turned her head to see Boone Harrison flanking Nick. With a tip of his hat, he pointed toward the podium. "You heard the lady. The press conference is over there."

Vanessa Owen puffed up inside her suit. "Sheriff Harrison, you're not even a member of KCPD."

"You know I'm the last person you want to be messin' with, Ms. Owen." The sheriff's low drawl hinted at some secret tension that existed between them. "Now you show Dr. Kilpatrick and this fine young lady the respect they deserve."

Perhaps thinking better of trying to get past both Nick and Boone Harrison, Vanessa's mouth dipped with a pouty sigh. She drew her fingers across her throat, telling her irate cameraman to cut the feed. One by one the mob turned away. The elevator dinged behind them and Annie exhaled an audible sigh of relief. With a nod to Nick, Boone Harrison and the two other officers herded Vanessa

Owen and the rest of the group back to the far side of the lobby.

The elevator doors slid open and Nick ushered Annie inside.

But there was one more flash of a camera. She recognized Gabriel Knight's black hair and blue eyes from a task force briefing. The man had been particularly critical of the task force's lack of progress on the case in the column he wrote for one of the local papers. He stood outside the open doors, tipping his head toward the injury on her forehead. "Somebody got to you, didn't they, Ms. Hermann? Are you certain it wasn't *him?*"

Nick punched the door close button. "No comment."

The doors shut on the nightmarish episode. Maybe she should stop clinging to the idea that anything about her life would ever be *normal* again.

She jumped at the touch of Nick's hand folding over hers where she squeezed the back railing. "Easy. You okay?"

Annie stared straight ahead at the doors, desperately trying to organize the thoughts and emotions that had jumbled inside her. "I am a well-trained scientist with multiple university degrees. I've worked at the lab for three years now. I find facts. I solve crimes. I'm good at what I do."

"I know."

She was vaguely aware of the elevator rising beneath her feet. "All those people wanted something from me. I hate being in the spotlight like that. I get tongue-tied. I can't think straight. This is exactly why I'm a lab geek. I don't want to be on the front page of anything. I just want to do my job." An instinct she barely recognized and scarcely trusted prompted her to release the railing and turn her palm into Nick's. As unsettling and ill-timed her attraction to him might be, he was solid and strong, and he'd been there for her these past twenty-four hours in ways no one had been there for her in ten long years. She held on tight and tilted her eyes to his. "How do they know it was me at that crime scene? How does anyone know?"

He didn't stop at holding hands this time. Before she got her questions out, he was pulling her up to his chest and wrapping his arms around her. "I don't know. Other than my partner and your boss, no one should know you pulled that assignment. I haven't even filed my report yet."

"I worked with Raj Kapoor at the lab yesterday. He knows."

"Would he talk?"

Annie shook her head. "He's a friend. We started together at the lab at the same time. He wouldn't hurt me."

"Maybe not intentionally. Is he a chatty guy?"

Annie shrugged. "To be honest, I guess I don't know him that well outside of work. He *is* on his phone a lot, but I've never seen him talking with reporters."

"There are also our fake cops, Gobel and Ramirez."

"Either of them could have talked to Vanessa Owen." Inhaling the leathery scent that was uniquely Nick's, Annie burrowed her head beneath his chin and circled her arms around his waist. "I thought I heard him again, Nick. The man on the phone. That voice from the alley. He called me Annabelle."

"Just now? You heard it here?"

"Maybe I imagined it. Maybe my fear is getting the better of my common sense." She turned her ear to the strong beat of his heart, loving the way his shoulders curved around her. "Do you think that voice on the phone is someone working with the rapist? Was he driving that car that nearly hit us? Do you think he killed Rachel? Do you think one of those reporters knows who attacked me? Or, even worse, knows who the Rose Red Rapist is?"

"Always with the questions, eh, slugger?" Nick pulled the stocking cap from her hair and tunneled his fingers into the curls at her nape, gently massaging her there.

"That's because I need answers. I feel like I'm in limbo until I know something for sure."

"We'll get them." His heat warmed her. His strength gave her strength. His teasing diverted her attention from her futile speculation and she realized she'd been shaking. Hard. But Nick was holding her, comforting her, letting her know she wasn't alone. "Give that brain of yours a rest for a couple of minutes. You're safe now, Annie. Nobody gets to bug you but me."

She hiccuped a laugh against his chest, relaxing into his embrace. The clever words sounded a lot like the old Nick, the adversary she was used to battling. But this Nick was still different. This Nick was serious. He was protective. He was tender. He wasn't the enemy.

This was the Nick she was falling in love with. Maybe the same Nick she'd had a thing for, for a long time now, only it had never made any sense for her to be attracted to a man so different from anyone or anything she knew. It would be too crazy, too dangerous to admit her awakening feelings for someone who claimed that guilt was the reason he'd suddenly become a part of her life.

But Nick made her feel safe.

That was one honest, irrefutable fact.

Another was their shared determination to find the truth. "I want those answers, Nick."

"Me, too." His hold on her didn't loosen until the elevator slowed its ascent. He released her entirely before the doors opened and they had to face coworkers, departmental protocol and a task force meeting. "I don't know how that information leaked to the press. But I intend to find out. I'm done chasing shadows."

Chapter Nine

Nick flipped his ink pen back and forth between his fingers, over and over, fighting that edgy need to do something that had fired through his blood for the past thirty-six hours. He was as restless and ready to work as the muscular German shepherd lying beside his handler's feet at the end of the conference room table. At least the dog got to pant and gnaw on his knotted rope to disperse some of that energy. Sitting through long meetings had never been Nick's favorite thing on the best of days, but everything about this morning's task force meeting reminded him of all the should-have-dones he'd mishandled since getting Spencer's phone call New Year's Eve.

He should have known Nell was sneaking out to see her bad-boy boyfriend.

He should have been in that alley with Annie to keep her from getting hurt and to protect the crucial evidence they'd lost.

He should have kept his hands to himself and never touched her, never kissed her, never got it into his head that sweet, soulful Annie Hermann was a lot more than the nerdy lab rat he had to work with on the task force.

Even now, he was having a hard time keeping his gaze from sliding across the table to watch her lift her coffee mug to those softly bowed lips that said a lot of smart stuff and tasted even better. His skin tingled with a remembered anticipation, watching her play with those natural, sable dark curls that had cupped and clung to his hands like silken fingers.

Annie pushed the tendrils off her face, frowning as she focused on the drawing set on the table in front of her. The subtle action exposed the bandage on her forehead, and the bruising that marred her porcelain skin. Nick could still feel her digging her fingers into his chest in that alley, feeling safer with him than without him. He could feel her wrapping her arms around his waist and holding on tight because a bunch of nosy reporters had caught her off guard and rattled her sense of security. He could feel her deep inside, getting into his head, getting close to his heart.

He supposed an attraction must have been there all along, from that first task force meeting, when she'd spilled the contents of that loud paisley bag across the table and then clumsily gathered up the mess with an apology that made him think she was all innocence and way out of her league. Yet, ten minutes later, she'd been thumping the table, challenging him head-to-head about her science beating his street smarts. It was hard not to notice someone like that.

Her petite height made her a perfect fit for his vertically challenged frame. But with those eyes and that hair, she could have been six-feet tall and his hormones would still be firing on all cylinders. How could a woman look so barely thrown together and yet exude such an earthy sexuality? How could she be so intellectual and stubborn and emotionally guarded, and still be soft and witty and so easy to kiss?

Maybe that was why they'd been butting heads for so long. He liked her. More than he should. And just what exactly did they have in common besides working together and loving baseball? It made no damn sense.

"Would you agree, Nick?"

He nearly snapped the pen in half as Spencer Montgomery's voice cut through the rising tide of Nick's emotions. He carefully placed the instrument on the table top instead, buying himself a second to shuffle his thoughts to catch up with the conversation in the third-floor conference room. They were looking at a drawing of the alleged accomplice to the man who'd attacked Annie.

"This is the sketch Officers Galbreath and Foster gave us of the fake cop who relieved them of duty at the Shamrock Bar. They never saw the second impostor." Spencer, the task force leader, sat at the head of the table. As his partner, Nick always sat at the corner beside him. "Based on his height and the pot belly Galbreath described, Annie thinks it has to be the other guy who stole and destroyed our evidence."

Nick zeroed in on the computer-generated image sitting in front of him and the details the two KCPD officers had described. Receding blond hair. Five-nine. Nick pushed the paper away. "He has to be the getaway driver. The man I chased was six-two, six-three."

Add in the bulk of his parka, and the man had been nearly twice the size of Annie. She was lucky to have survived the attack.

But when Nick looked across the table to tell her so, he saw her turning the page of a lab report, poring over the information, as oblivious to the conversation now as he'd been a moment ago. Unlike him, however, from the way she worked her lips into a frown, and skipped back and forth from one data-filled printout to the next, he doubted she was contemplating the relationship—or whatever this was—growing between them.

Spencer, fortunately, was as focused on the case as ever. He nodded to the red-haired officer in her navy blue uniform sitting beside Nick as she typed notes on her laptop. "Maggie, add that to the BOLO we've got out on those two guys."

"Yes, sir." After typing in the updates, Sergeant Maggie Wheeler repeated the details to the group.

"Balding blond man. Blue or green eyes. Five-nine to five-ten. Heavyset. Second unsub is six-two to six-three. Large frame. Both in fake KCPD uniforms—which I'm sure neither one will still be wearing," she added as an aside before going back to the details of her report. "Big man wore black parka with dark stocking mask over face."

"Brown eyes." The image suddenly gelled in Nick's memory as he replayed the chase through the alley. "I couldn't see much else about the guy with the mask he wore. But when I took a bead on him, brown eyes were looking back at me."

"Would you concur, Annie?"

"What?" Annie's head shot up and her eyes blinked several times at Sergeant Wheeler while she processed the question the redhead had asked. "Yes. His eyes were dark." Just as quickly as she'd looked up from her printouts, though, she turned her attention to them again. But her fingers scratched at her throat and she kept talking. "He had a funny voice, too—like he had laryngitis. Maybe he was short of breath or disguising his voice, but there was no tone to it."

And then she was completely immersed in the files again.

Maggie grinned at the offhand, yet precise, detail, and typed. "Raspy voice. I'll add that to the suspect description and get copies sent out to all the precincts."

The protective adrenaline inside Nick pumped up

a notch. Annie thought her attacker and the crank caller were the same man—and that he had spoken to her down in the lobby during that mob of a press conference. She'd dismissed it as fear and imagination. But he wasn't so sure there was anything imaginary about it. Annie didn't trust her own instincts that way.

But Nick did.

Brown eyes. He'd gotten no more than a fleeting glance in a shadowed alley before the perp had grabbed his loot and run out of sight around the corner. And it was possible he was transposing Jordan Garza's brown eyes in his memory, because the teen was equally high on his list of threats he wanted to get off the streets.

But his gut was telling him that that detail was something important. Now if he could just get his gut to clarify the relevance of that memory—put the eyes to a face, pin that voice to a particular man—then they might actually make some progress on this investigation.

Although Nick couldn't pinpoint where yet, he'd looked into those eyes more than once. Only in passing—not enough for their shape and color to register at the time. But he'd seen them someplace besides that alley. He'd seen Annie's attacker.

If he could just place the bastard. Nick would have that guy in handcuffs so fast, he'd be in lockup before he even knew he'd been arrested. Annie would be safe. Nick could get off this damn guilt trip. And then maybe they could go back to square one, and see if something between them really could work without the threats and the job and the task force affecting everything they said or did.

Nick sensed his partner's cool gray eyes glancing his way, and he realized he was flipping that stupid pen between his fingers again. Wisely tucking it away inside the neckline of the layered thermal shirts he wore, Nick turned his attention back to the table.

"Moving on," Spencer continued. "Fortunately, Nick and Annie were able to recover photographs of the scene as well as some blood evidence." He nodded to the CSI who'd now lined up three reports side by side to peruse them. "Annie?"

"This can't be right," she muttered, scanning from one report to the other.

"Annie?"

She lifted her chin and looked around as though surprised to see her colleagues at the table with her.

Spencer leaned back in his chair and needlessly smoothed the knot on his tie. "You said you had a serology report?"

"Yeah. Yes." *Earth to Sherlock*. The taunt was poised on the tip of Nick's tongue, but he couldn't say it. Forty-eight hours ago, he'd have called her a space cadet for being so distracted. But now all he could see were the wheels turning inside her head, piecing together information with a precision his gut envied.

"Did you come up with something?" he asked instead.

Annie's golden-brown eyes found his across the table. The cautious excitement he read there lit an answering current of energy inside him. "If I hadn't completed these tests myself, I'd tell the techs to rerun them. But I think we just caught a break. A big one."

"Explain," Spencer ordered.

The electricity she was giving off blazed up another notch as she turned to include every task force member around the table. "I haven't had a chance to make copies yet, so I'll pass these around. The photograph shows two handprints on the alley wall—one man-sized, and a smaller one which matches Rachel Dunbar's hand." She passed the files to Kate Kilpatrick beside her. "The blood samples Nick and I saved were too degraded to get a DNA profile, but I can confirm the blood in those handprints came from two separate donors."

"A man and a woman." Kate scanned the files before handing them off to the big-shouldered K-9 officer, Pike Taylor, sitting at the end of the table. "I'm assuming one of them belongs to the victim?" she asked.

"Most likely. The M.E.'s report types Rachel Dunbar's blood as O positive. One of my samples was also O positive."

Pike glanced at the files before passing them on to Maggie. "This says 'Unknown Donor.' So who does the other blood belong to?"

Annie looked to Officer Taylor and shrugged. "Like I said, the samples were too degraded to get an exact match to anyone in the system. But that second sample is O negative."

"Does that mean what I think it does?" Maggie asked, pushing the reports on to Nick.

Nick understood. "Our unsub has O negative blood."

Believing in absolute proof, Spencer raised a cautious hand, tempering the sidebar conversations and beginnings of a celebration around the table. "Are you sure it's the rapist's blood, and not the accomplice's who came to clean up the place after him?"

Annie stood and leaned over the table to slide the files in front of the task force leader. Then she pointed to a paragraph in the top report. "Look at the time line. The blood spatter and handprints I found behind the Dumpster had been there longer—by three or four hours—than the blood farther back in the alley where the victim died. Rachel Dunbar fought back when she was abducted—maybe she even saw her attacker's face. But she got a piece of him—scratched him, knocked him into the wall, hit him with something, who knows? The rapist may have washed her clothes and sterilized her body, removing any trace of himself off the victim. But he was bleeding in that alley, and he left a part of himself on that wall." Once Spencer nodded his agreement, she sat back in her chair. "The Rose Red Rapist has O negative blood."

Spencer jotted the information in his notebook, making it a fact he believed, moving their case forward. "That fits Kate's profile about two unsubs— the man responsible for the rapes and the 'cleaner' who comes in after him to mop up any mistakes."

Nick could feel that they were finally on the right track. "If the rapist was injured in his blitz attack, that also explains why his sidekick upped his involvement to murder. Either Rachel Dunbar saw his face and had to be silenced, or he wanted some kind of retribution for hurting his...*idol,* for want of a better word."

"So we're looking for an unsub with O negative blood," Annie concluded. "And one or more people who clean up after him."

Spencer took the suspect analysis one step further. "Our unsub either has a lot of money to pay this cleanup crew for their help and silence—"

"—or there's a relationship of some kind between them." Nick was feeling more like his old self, more like the detective he'd been before the turn of the New Year. "One that ensures loyalty— through blackmail, bribery, family ties, whatever."

"Our unsub profiles are taking shape. We've got some specifics to look for that we haven't had before," Spencer agreed. He pulled a sheet of paper from his notebook before closing it, indicating the meeting was almost at an end—meaning they could all get back to tracking down these lowlife scumbags who preyed on women in the city. "Good work, Hermann."

"Nick, too," she insisted, beaming at their supervisor's simple praise. "I wouldn't have come away with any evidence if it wasn't for him."

"Nah." Nick waved off the compliments directed at him, suspecting they could have come away with so much more if he'd truly been doing his job in that alley. He was proud of Annie's eye for details and thorough deduction, and put the credit where it was due. "This is all on you, slugger."

"Enough with the mutual-admiration society." Spencer's authoritative voice silenced the chatter in the room. "We're glad you're here with us, period, Annie. All right, people, just because this is the first break we've had in months doesn't mean we've solved the case. It's not like we'll get warrants to test every man in Kansas City who has O negative blood. We still have work to do." The sobering reminder dulled the gold in Annie's eyes, and she busied herself with closing up the lab reports and putting them in her bag. "Pike, any luck tracking down the E-14 parking sticker?"

"Not yet." The big man on their team gave a succinct report. "I did some work with the picture Annie took, but even at high resolution, it's too dark and blurry to get a plate number or the

name of an apartment complex or workplace off
the sticker. I can tell you the car was a Chevy Suburban, recent make. Black with silver mag wheels.
Patrols will be on the lookout for a car matching
that description with a green-and-white sticker."
Pike turned to direct the last of his information
directly to Nick. "I've also arranged for security
patrols to make hourly drive-bys around Annie's
apartment, like you asked."

For a moment, Nick wondered if he'd overstepped his authority by making the private request before the meeting. But after the late-night
call, the near miss with the car and the frenzy of
this morning's press conference, he wasn't taking
any chances with Annie's safety.

Her eyes rounded. "That isn't necessary."

"Yeah, it is." Nick wasn't going to apologize for
singling her out for the extra security. "I've only
had a couple hours of shut-eye over the past forty-
eight, so I have a feeling I'm going to crash hard
tonight—but I don't want to leave you unprotected."

"Nick." She tried to hush him. "You have re-
sponsibilities at home. You need to be there." Her
gaze darted around the table, taking in the knowing, concerned expressions of the other task force
members, before coming back to communicate a
warning to him.

He braced his elbows on the table and leaned toward her, ignoring the silent reprimand. "You don't
think these people know where I was last night?"

Her cheeks dotted with a pink blush, then began to pale before she looked away. He couldn't tell if she was embarrassed to learn the others knew she'd had a man in her apartment, or that they might think she couldn't take care of herself. He wasn't going to apologize for the former, and he didn't think that anyone here, under normal circumstances, believed the latter. But these weren't normal circumstances.

Absorbing the brunt of her hurt and fury, Nick turned his attention to the rest of the room. While Annie remained his primary concern, he wasn't so shortsighted as to think she was the only one here who might have caught the eye of the unsubs they were after. "We don't know if this 'cleaner' guy is targeting Annie specifically, or if he'll come after the whole task force. But I don't think anyone here needs to make it easy for him. I recommend working with a partner or in groups anytime we're out in the field. And it needs to be with somebody we know has our back."

Pike's blue eyes narrowed. "You're worried about the fake cops coming back and infiltrating our investigation? We've got a face to look for now."

"For one man," Nick reminded him. "If these are hired goons, they'll just get somebody else—or use the man we didn't identify. The information's getting out somehow. The press knew about Annie's attack before we told them. I'm tired of these bastards having the upper hand on us. We need to close the circle."

Pike nodded, reaching down to pet the dog at his feet. "I've got Hans with me 24-7."

Maggie seemed to agree. "When I'm not working the desk here, I'm home with John and Travis." Her fiancé and son. From an incident with Maggie's abusive ex-husband the previous summer, Nick knew John Murdock—a former United States Marine—despite his disability, could supply the kind of backup Maggie would need away from the precinct. She pointed across the table. "And Kate's my maid of honor, so when I'm out planning the wedding, she's usually with me."

Spencer nodded his agreement. "Sounds like a smart idea. Kate, you can ask Sheriff Harrison to shadow you when he's in town, if he's willing."

"I'm sure he'll agree."

Nick and Spencer were partners, used to working calls together. That left Annie without any regular backup. But he didn't intend to leave the woman alone anytime soon. "You're with me, slugger," he promised. "If you're working any place outside the lab, I'm with you. Or else I'll make sure someone else from the task force is." He saw the protest forming on her lips and stopped it before it could start. "You know it makes sense."

"Okay," she answered dutifully, if without any enthusiasm, conceding the logic of his plan. "You and I are a team."

"That's the new rule for everybody, then," Spencer Montgomery announced. "Nobody works solo on this investigation. If you leave Precinct HQ or the lab for any reason on this case, backup goes with you. Nobody's out in the field on his or her own."

A chorus of *yes, sirs* rounded out the meeting, but Spencer didn't dismiss them. Instead he turned to Annie. "Are you up for another crime scene?"

"Of course."

Spencer held up the call sheet he'd pulled from his notebook and handed the address to Annie. "Then the last item on our agenda is a B and E call that came in early this morning."

"Breaking and entering?" Nick speared his partner with skeptical look. Was this the detective's idea of a task that would keep Annie out of harm's way? If so, he didn't know how single-minded about an investigation she could be. She'd find a way to get back into the mix, with or without Spencer's permission.

"Relax, partner," the red-haired detective assured him. "There's an outside shot it could be related to our case." Nick should have known Spencer didn't do or say anything without thinking it through first. "This particular break-in happened last night in a building in the same neighborhood where Rachel Dunbar was murdered and the other rape victims were abducted. There's no report of anything being taken, or in fact, any crime beyond the vandalism, but it's on an upper floor where the old warehouse is being renovated into offices and condos."

"A construction site," said Annie, seeing the same possibility Nick did. The last surviving victim of the Rose Red Rapist described being taken to a building that was either being renovated or newly built. "Do you really think our unsub would be so careless as to leave evidence behind in two different locations?"

Kate Kilpatrick offered the profiler's perspective on the possibility. "If Rachel Dunbar saw his face or injured him in some way, then his routine had already been compromised. This guy's compulsive enough that the change in his attack strategy could trigger some kind of psychotic break. His control could be unraveling, leading to a chain of mistakes and erratic behavior."

Nick rolled his chair back from the table and stood. "It could just be that some partiers were looking for a private place to get drunk and keep the New Year's celebration rolling."

Pike Taylor was on his feet, too. "Might be a homeless guy trying to get out of the cold."

Annie downed the last of her coffee and shrugged into the sleeves of her black wool coat. "If nothing else, we can at least prove the rape *didn't* happen there. Right?"

"Exactly." Spencer stood and buttoned his suit jacket, signaling the end of the task force meeting.

"Sorry to cut your holidays short, everyone. Let's get to work. Dismissed."

Kate put a hand on Annie's arm, stopping her on her way out the door. "Could I see you in my office? I'm responsible for the well-being of everyone here. I want to chat with you for a few minutes about the assault."

"But the crime scene—"

"I'll make it fast."

"Sure." With a cautioning glance over her shoulder to Nick, maybe wondering if he'd leave without her, maybe wondering if the psychologist would ask what had happened at her apartment *after* the attack, Annie looped that ridiculously pink carryall bag over her neck and shoulder and followed Kate out to the hallway.

Nick threw his coat on and hurried around the table to catch them, wanting to reassure her that he meant it when he said he'd be there for her. He waited for Pike and his dog, and Maggie Wheeler to precede him out the door.

And then he stood face-to-face with his partner, who pushed the door shut.

"Give me a minute before you go," Spencer said, casually sitting on the edge of the conference table.

Nick's muscles leaped with the instinct to open the door and go after Annie. He curled his fingers into his palms instead, dredging up a grin to mask the impulse. His partner never did anything casually. There had to be a reason for this private conversation. "What's up?"

"Slugger?"

One slip. One stinking little slip. So Spencer had zeroed in on the connection between him and Annie in the space of an hour, when it had taken Nick months to realize that CSI Hermann meant a hell of a lot more to him than a simple coworker should. Probably why his partner was the senior detective. Still, Nick wasn't comfortable spelling it out for Spencer when he hadn't yet figured out where this thing with Annie was headed himself. He took one shot at blowing it off as no big deal.

Nick shrugged. "I found out she was a baseball fan. Figured that was a nicer nickname than Brainiac or Space Cadet."

Spencer didn't buy a word of it. "This is from one partner, one friend, to another. What's going on with you and Hermann?"

"Nothing." Plan B: Admit a little. Keep everything else close to the vest. "I'm working through some guilt over her getting hurt and not being where I should have been to save that evidence from being taken." He reached for the doorknob. "I promised her protection. I intend to deliver. I can't do it from here."

"Nice speech, but this is me you're talking to. You weren't focused at the meeting—"

"I haven't had much sleep. Nell's dating this nightmare—"

"You couldn't keep your eyes off her." His perceptive gaze dropped to the fist at Nick's side. "Right now you're about to crawl out of your skin because she's out of your sight. That's more than guilt—or a bodyguard doing his job. What's going on?"

Ah, hell. Nick raked his fingers through his hair and paced to the end of the room. If he couldn't tell his partner—the man he trusted most in this world—then who could he talk to about this craziness? "I kissed her." He turned to face him. "Twice."

Spencer just sat there, betraying no reaction one way or the other. Nick had seen him use the tactic countless times in interrogation rooms, waiting in expectant silence until the perp got so uncomfortable he started spilling his guts. The damn tactic worked.

"I'd have taken her to bed, too, if we hadn't got interrupted by that crank phone call last night." Nick paced back, pointing to the door. "Somebody thinks she's the weak link on this investigation. They're targeting her. They've got her number. They know where she lives. And it's my fault. I'm the one who let her get hurt. I'm the one who left her exposed and put her on The Cleaner's radar."

"You kissed her?" Spencer smirked, the equivalent of a big, teasing grin on any other man.

"Come on, Spence. Focus on what's important here."

"I am." The smirk disappeared and he pushed to

his feet. "Your objectivity has been compromised. You're already distracted by whatever's going on with your family, and now you've got the hots for Annie?"

"It doesn't mean I can't do my job. I'm still a good cop."

"One of the best I've ever known. I know there's nobody I'd rather have out on the street backing me up."

Nick shrugged off the compliment that went both ways. "She doesn't have any backup, Spence. I've never seen anyone go through the world as alone as that woman does."

"So all that weirdness between you two was because you feel obligated to her. The kisses were just your way of welcoming in the New Year and meant nothing to you. I can assign someone else to protect her."

"No." Okay, so that answer was a little too emphatic to prove his objectivity.

Instead of calling him on the proprietary outburst, Spencer moved back to the head of the table to gather his notebook and coffee mug, remaining as unflappable as ever. "So why did you kiss her?"

Because he'd needed to. Because standing even a few inches away from Annie last night had been too far away. Everything inside him—the guilt, the worry, the compassion, the frustration—had centered and calmed the moment she'd put her hand on his chest. All night and day his raw nerves and beat-up emotions had been sparking through him like a disconnected power line. But when Annie had touched him, when they'd kissed, the circuit found completion—and the electricity he felt every time he was around her had hummed smoothly, powerfully inside him—through both of them.

But he wasn't sharing that fanciful notion with anybody, not even his partner. "Is there a purpose to this conversation? Or are you jealous because you've got no personal life, so you're interfering with mine? If you need some attention, Grandma Connie still wants to adopt you."

Spencer laughed, allowing him that one dig. "Hey, I might take her up on that offer one day with the way she cooks. But right now I need you and Annie focused on this investigation."

"Let her focus. I'll keep her safe," Nick promised. "I won't screw up again."

And then the laughter was done. "I'm not questioning your abilities. Maybe your judgment, a little bit. You know I lost someone I was protecting."

"I know, buddy." It was a piece of Spencer's past that few people knew about. It was a testament to their bond that Spencer had shared the story during one late-night stakeout. "I can't imagine what you went through when your witness got killed."

"It'll gut you, Nick. In more ways than you can imagine." A shadow darkened Spencer's features for a split second, reminding Nick that the woman

Spencer had been protecting had been far more than a witness to him.

The painful fist of possibility punched Nick in the gut. He couldn't imagine holding a lifeless Annie in his arms and going on with life the way Spencer had. And maybe that, more than anything else, confirmed that whatever he felt for her was real, and strong.

Nick nodded, appreciating the heartfelt advice. "I won't let my feelings get in the way of doing my job. But I don't want this job to get in the way of something that might be pretty good."

Erasing the aftereffects of that past tragedy from his expression, Spencer came around the table again. "I'll give you credit—you've always been braver than me in that department. Maybe not smarter, but always braver. I just don't want to see either of you get hurt. On the job or off."

"Tell *her* that. You know me, I don't dink around when something feels right." He squeezed his fists in frustration, needing to pace off this restless energy again. "But she's so blow hot, blow cold—all 'need and hold me' one minute, and 'let's play by the rules' the next. And it's not a game with her. I think she's so damn scared of getting hurt that she doesn't want to believe we could have something." Nick stopped in his tracks. "Maybe it's just me she doesn't believe in."

"Then she doesn't know you like I do. Give her time to figure it out."

"You think she will?"

Spencer's shoulders lifted in an uncharacteristic shrug. "Look, I'm the last one to give anybody relationship advice. But I can tell you that, technically, there's no conflict of interest in you two hooking up. She works for the lab and you're KCPD, so you aren't breaking any protocol rules."

"That's just a small part of it. But thanks for the ammunition. It's tough to win an argument with that woman."

The smirk came back. "Then maybe you ought to quit arguing and kiss her a third time."

"That's your advice? Stick to being a cop, Romeo." Nick grinned and opened the door. "I'll keep my priorities straight. Now let me get to work."

Spencer followed him out. "Call if you need anything, with Annie or Nell. And watch your back. I expect to see you both at the next briefing."

Nick waved over his shoulder as he headed down the hallway to Dr. Kilpatrick's office. But when he walked past the maze of detectives' work stations in the third floor's center room, he saw his uncle sitting at his desk, and changed course. "What are you doing here?"

George Madigan, dressed in his suit-and-tie best, rose from Nick's chair to greet him with a handshake. "Good morning to you, too."

"Sorry." Nick answered his uncle's teasing smile

and tossed his gloves and the break-in report on his desk. "It's been a long morning. How are you?"

"Ready for a nap." It was a joke. Despite the gray that peppered his hair, George's sturdy physique and coiled energy said he was fit and fine and up to something. "Like you, I've been sitting in a long meeting—talking with Precinct Chief Taylor about the task force budget. Because I was in the neighborhood, I thought I'd stick around to see if you were up for lunch."

"I can't. I've got a B and E call I need to get to." But Nick was more concerned about his uncle's passing comment than he was about missing lunch. "You and Chief Taylor were talking about the task force?"

"Thought you might pick up on that."

Feeling the need to go on the defensive, Nick pulled back the front of his jacket and propped his hands at his hips. "Are you cutting our funding?"

"Money's always tight at the beginning of the year. Actually, though, I'm looking for reasons to justify increasing your budget. The Rose Red Rapist is a top-priority case for KCPD. Terrible PR for the department until we arrest someone. Naturally, the commissioner wants the case solved sooner rather than later, so we're looking for ways to help your team do that." George draped his long coat through the crook of his arm and perched on the corner of his desk. "Any new information? Any breaks in the case you can give me without waiting for it to go through channels to my office?"

Nick relaxed his stance. "We just had a break-through, thanks to Annie. We got a blood type on our perp. The task force is certain we're looking for two unsubs now. We don't believe the rapist has escalated to killing his victims."

"That *is* good news."

"We're looking at an accomplice—someone the rapist knows or even a sicko fan who thinks he's doing him a favor—as the actual murderer. We've nicknamed the second unsub The Cleaner."

"Just the kind of sound bite the press will have a field day with." George groaned at the idea, but kept the conversation focused on business. "So you're expanding the investigation to look for two unsubs?"

"At least. We've got two perps we want to track down for impersonating police officers. One could be the killer—one could be the rapist. Or they could be hired help."

George's gray eyes narrowed. "Instead of zero-ing in on a suspect, it sounds like the task force is expanding the scope of its investigation."

Nick nodded. "Any connection we can bust gets us one step closer to finding the bastard."

"So cutting funding for your investigation couldn't come at a worse time."

"Duh." The deputy commissioner had asked the question, but Nick pleaded with his mom's brother.

"Pull some strings, George. Help us. Don't let the brass and budget cuts hinder our investigation."

George stood and shook open his coat. "Let me know as soon as you make one of those connections that gives us a break on this case, and I'll do everything in my power to make sure your task force has what it needs—manpower, equipment, you name it."

"Thanks. You'll know something when I do."

As effortlessly as he buttoned his coat and pulled his scarf and gloves from his pockets, George switched to a new topic. "How's the girl?"

"Annie?"

"Yes." His uncle winked. "The CSI you spent the night with last night."

"On her couch, George. I slept on her couch." Not that every cell in his body hadn't wanted to climb into that bed where she'd been playing possum and hold her so that they both could sleep. "She looks a little worse for wear, but she's fine. Annie's a small package, but she's tough."

"Good to hear." George draped his navy blue scarf around his neck. "I suppose I should give you a heads-up that your mother is planning on paying the two of you a visit tonight. Trudy says she and the girls are on a knitting kick today, and Connie's making another pot of minestrone. Apparently she was quite a hit at breakfast."

His gut warned him that Annie needed to take his family in small doses if he didn't want to scare her off a relationship before it ever got started. But his brain latched on to a more important detail. "So Nell is hanging out at home today?"

"I don't know if it's by choice, but at least that Garza boy hasn't been back to the house. Your father filled me in."

"Yeah. Apparently, Nell opened up to Annie and talked about Garza grilling her about me, and losing his temper." Nick shook his head in frustration. "Maybe Annie's patience and ability to reason are the way to get Nell to see sense and dump the guy. Lord knows my efforts haven't done any good."

George slapped his leather gloves into his palm and made a fist. "I know I'm not a front-line cop anymore, but I looked up the current roster on suspected associates of the 7th Street Snakes. Gang Squad says Garza was brought in for questioning a couple of times this past year—for jacking car parts and assault. But he was never charged with anything."

"So Nell's right? If he's not in the gang anymore, though, why ask about me?" But he didn't feel any relief when he saw the grim expression lining his uncle's face. "What?"

"Jordan Garza is still a member, according to their sources. Even more than that, they suspect he's being groomed to become one of Ramon Sanchez's lieutenants. He may be using Nell to get Gang Squad information he thinks you have."

Nick swore, shoving his fingers through his hair

in lieu of punching his fist through the side of his desk. "And he put his hands on my sister? I don't suppose you could pull some strings and park a black-and-white by the house to make sure Garza and his Impala don't show up in the neighborhood again?"

"Already done." George reached out and squeezed Nick's shoulder before checking his watch and pulling away. "I'd better grab some lunch and get back to the office. I'm interviewing potential new assistants this afternoon. An administrator's work is never done." He sighed and pulled on his gloves. "Keep me in the loop on the task force's progress, all right?"

"Will do. Keep me in the loop if anything else happens at home I need to know about."

"I will." He'd taken only a couple of steps toward the elevator when he stopped and smiled. "CSI Hermann. Or may I call you Annie?"

Nick had already identified Annie's arrival by her unique lavender-and-soap scent when he turned to run interference if needed.

"Hello, sir."

His uncle shook his head. "Still need to work on that *sir* stuff."

"Right." She twisted her fingers around the thick strap of her purse. "Good to see you…George."

"See? That didn't hurt, did it?"

A wry smile crept across her lips. "Not as much as the last time."

With a laugh that relaxed Nick's concern, George walked away. "Bye, Annie."

Nick was still marveling at this woman's resilience when she tilted her face up to his. "Are you ready?"

"Everything go okay with Dr. Kilpatrick?"

"I'm no more eccentric than usual. She gave me her number—told me to call anytime. She advised me to surround myself with people I trust..." Oh, man. That must have echoed around that empty hole of grief she carried with her. Before Nick could come up with the right words to reassure her she wasn't alone, she unwound her fingers from her purse and reached up to brush some rumpled spikes of his hair off his forehead. An intimate heat sparked through him at the shy caress. "Everything okay with your family?"

One little touch and he was a changed man. *Oh, yeah, Spencer was right. As usual.* Nick's objectivity regarding Annie Hermann was sorely compromised.

He nodded. "For now."

Energized, humbled, eager to spend time with this woman and ready to work, Nick grabbed his stuff off his desk. Resisting the urge to grab her hand amid the public hubbub of cops and criminals and staff moving around the room, he turned her toward the elevator. "Let's go find some evidence."

Chapter Ten

Regina Hollister could go a little easy on the perfume, Annie thought, as she and Nick rode the elevator up to the fourth floor of the old St. James Brothers Textiles warehouse building. Or maybe that was her boss's cologne that made Annie's eyes water in the enclosed space.

Brian Elliott, the owner of the building, had insisted on meeting the police here himself to inspect the damage done to his latest investment. The two executives could have been twins, with their charcoal-gray suits and wool dress coats. They both towered over Annie, both had dark hair, and both probably made more money in a week than she and Nick combined earned in a year as public servants. At least, that's what the tailored clothes, Rolex and expensive scents seemed to indicate.

As the elevator car slowed to a stop, Annie heard a banging sound from the floor above her, giving her an uneasy feeling. And as they stopped and the doors opened, she was hit with a new barrage of scents—sawdust, mold, hot metal, chemicals.

At the screech of a power saw blade hitting wood, Annie pushed her way off the elevator first and surveyed the ten or twelve construction workers.

She had to raise her voice to be heard over the pounding of hammers and conversations among the men. "Please tell me this isn't our crime scene." This was as bad a situation for contamination as the winter storm had been. "With all this traffic and dust, there's no way we'll find any usable evidence. Where are the officers who are supposed to cordon off the scene?"

"Watch out." Nick pulled her back a step as a man dressed in tan coveralls strode by with a stack of treated lumber balanced on his shoulder. Nick glanced up at the building's owner for an explanation. "Mr. Elliott?"

"This is what progress looks like." The wealthy man seemed almost entranced by the bustle of activity around them. "Men are working. I'm saving something old and beautiful. We're creating a useful space here."

The last person to exit the elevator, Regina Hollister, touched her boss's sleeve and turned him toward the west wall. Thankfully, her response was more practical. "This is as high as the public elevator goes. The break-in happened one floor above us. We'll have to take the stairs." She walked around the power tools and workmen, expecting the rest of them to follow. "This way."

They met two uniformed cops standing at the

base of a concrete stairwell. The openings going both up and down had been wrapped in plastic, although Annie noted that neither entry had been completely sealed, allowing easy enough access to the floors above and below them.

Nick was more interested in the two uniforms, a man and a woman. "Let me see your IDs and badges." He made sure badge numbers and pictures checked out before dismissing them. "Wait downstairs. I'll call if we need anything."

The crinkling of plastic being pushed aside and the high-pitched whistle of the winter wind blowing through a broken window were the only sounds on the fifth floor. The layers of plastic and thick floor muffled the sounds of the workmen beneath their feet. Nick lifted the yellow crime scene tape at the top of the stairs and the group stepped into a cavernous space of concrete and history.

"This entire floor is the crime scene?" Annie frowned. Processing this much space was almost as daunting as working through the chaos downstairs.

Regina Hollister pointed to the opposite wall. "The break-in happened over there, but because the workmen aren't finished with this level yet, the officers didn't want anyone coming up here."

"These stairs are the only access point?" Nick asked, pulling out his notebook to jot down information.

"They were," Regina answered. She pointed to the only relatively solid wall, where broken boards and caution tape revealed glimpses of the iron work behind them. "There's the old freight elevator, but it's been boarded up for decades behind that wall. The building inspector says it's not structurally safe."

"But we intend to bring it back up to code," Brian Elliott added, still focused more on the renovation than the crime that had happened here. "Once we refinish the wrought-iron and brass trims, we think it will be a real selling point—a truly unique entrance to the two-story penthouse my people are designing for this floor and the one above us."

Setting her purse down beside her kit, Annie pulled a pair of sterile gloves from the CSI vest she wore, and readied to go to work. She opened her kit to retrieve her camera and loop it around her neck, and then pulled out her flashlight. Although there was enough natural light coming through the windows to see the general layout of the place, she shined her light from one corner to the next for a closer inspection.

It did look as though Brian Elliott's crew was in the midst of gutting the old textile factory. New windows had been installed in the exterior walls, which had been taken down to the original red brick. Crisscrossing through the middle were exposed two-by-fours, some wrapped in plastic to protect the old wiring inside, others framing heating and exhaust ducts that ran from the concrete floor to the ceiling and through the rafters overhead. Fluorescent paint marked holes where toilets and plumbing had been removed, and a path had been sprayed from the stairs to a Dumpster chute where a window used to be. In front of that lay a scattered mess of debris, from vintage wooden spools that had once held miles of thread and skeins of material to a broken-down mattress and discarded rolls of plastic.

"Did these used to be apartments?" Annie asked, lowering her light to take a few wide-angle shots.

Brian Elliott came up beside her to answer. "Over the years the warehouse storage spaces were sectioned off into tiny apartments. We're opening it up and converting it into loft condominiums, reserving the bottom floor for office or business space."

"So you're working from the top floor down," Nick clarified. With his father's expertise as a contractor, he probably knew a lot about the work going on here. "Replacing windows, taking out non-load-bearing walls, bringing wiring up to code."

Annie expanded her search, taking more photos while Brian Elliott talked about his grand plan for renovating the historic building.

"We're also adding central heating and air. But that won't come in until the second phase." He pointed to a space heater next to a framed-up wall. "In the meantime we're using space heaters to keep the temperature tolerable for the workers and clients who come to see their potential future investment."

After a nod of permission from Annie, Nick followed the line to the broken window and peered out. "The fire escape is right here. I'm guessing a homeless person. After that storm, they'd be drawn to the heat and a place out of the wind. Annie?" He called her over to inspect the mattress tossed in front of one of the space heaters. "Whoever broke in probably pulled it out of the trash to sleep on."

Pulling out the ultraviolet attachment and goggles for her flashlight, she took note of the stains, both human and otherwise, that decorated the old mattress. "The last surviving witness said she came to on a mattress at a building under construction. That the rape took place there before he returned her to the abduction site."

"But our guy's a neat freak." Some of the construction plastic has been cut off the walls and folded over the end of the mattress like a blanket. Annie snapped a picture before Nick moved aside the plastic and shook the dust off it. "Even if he covered it with plastic, do you think he'd want to mess with this trash heap?"

"I don't know." Annie ran through witness accounts from previous attacks and tried to make them match what she was seeing here. *Close, but not quite* counted when playing horseshoes, but not in a forensic investigation. "This is weird," she confessed, drawing on the instincts that served Nick so well. "I feel like this has been staged. It has elements of the attacks, but it isn't quite right."

"It's another one of those damn coincidences I

don't like." Maybe she was rubbing off on him, too. "I'd rather see some cold, hard facts."

"Maybe this is just a break-in."

"You're just getting started," he reminded her, going back to the window. "Let's not make any decisions yet. Footprints in the snow out there. Your intruder came up from the outside. Probably climbed up until he found a window where he could force his way in."

Annie tipped up one of the giant spools and climbed up on it to inspect the window inside and out. "So where did our intruder go after spending the night? All I see are tracks leading in—nothing going back down the fire escape."

"Maybe he sneaked down the stairs and out the front door after the construction crew opened up the place this morning."

"Looks like he tried to pry the window open first, lost patience and then broke through the pane with a—" she followed the trail of broken glass across the floor with her flashlight and recoiled with a gasp "—a brick."

She caught Nick's worried gaze looking up at her and shook off his concern. It was another ugly coincidence, nothing more. "The brick used to kill Rachel Dunbar was stained with her blood," she reminded him. "There's nothing but a lot of dust on that one. No way is it the same murder weapon The Cleaner stole from me."

Still, it left her with the shivery feeling that there might be something more going on here than an innocent quest to get out of the cold. But Nick was right. She had to see everything first. Piece the clues together. Figure it out. And she needed to get rid of the audience across the room to do that.

"Annie? I'm here." An accented voice called to Annie from the stairs.

She glanced up to see Raj Kapoor push through the plastic barricade alongside another man in a suit and coat that matched Brian Elliott's. Surprise robbed her of breath and anchored her feet to the crate.

"What are *you* doing here?" She accepted Nick's outstretched hand to help her down, then held on to it a split second longer than was necessary to keep herself grounded in the moment at this surreal turn of events. But Annie was looking at the blond-haired man in the suit, not her coworker from the lab.

Nick's voice was an urgent whisper in her ear. "What's wrong? Doesn't the lab usually send backup when the crime scene's this big?"

"Adam?"

"Oh, my God. I saw you at the press conference on the noon news. Are you all right?" The tall blond in the suit walked straight across the marked path to Annie and scooped her up, camera and all, in a hug that lifted her right off her feet. "I didn't realize how badly you'd been hurt. It looks worse in person than it did—"

"Back it up, pal. You're interfering with a police investigation."

Annie saw Nick moving to block the embrace. He grasped the other man's arm and pried her free. Not a problem. She was already pushing against the unwanted, albeit familiar hug.

"And you are?" Adam lorded his six-foot-two status over Nick.

"It's all right." As soon as her toes touched the floor, Annie instinctively sought a place beside Nick to make the introductions at this awkward reunion. "Nick, this is Adam Matuszak. I...mentioned him, remember? This is Detective Nick Fensom."

"Matuszak." Nick rolled the name around his tongue. He folded his arms over his chest, creating a subtle barrier between her and Adam that seemed as much about staking territory as it did offering her protection from another hug.

"Detective."

Even though Adam extended his hand, Nick made no effort to take it. "So this is the guy who called you an odd duck."

"Excuse me?"

Annie pressed her lips together to stifle the urge to giggle. Nick *did* remember that brief conversation about her ex.

"It's a long story, Adam." She appreciated that

her ex-fiancé was still concerned for her well-being, but she was more annoyed that he'd traipsed across her crime scene. "What are you doing here?"

With his brown eyes narrowed in confusion, Adam curled his extended hand into a fist and dropped it to his side. "I'm Mr. Elliott's attorney. He wanted me here to make sure that no one was hurt at the break-in."

"So there'd be no liability claims?" Nick challenged.

"And no delays in the building's remodel. We've got tenants signed up to move in in the spring." Because he hadn't gotten the warm and fuzzy reception he must have expected from Annie, Adam slipped into rising-corporate-lawyer mode. "I'm not sure why two members of the Rose Red Rapist task force are here, either. Does this have something to do with your investigation? If so, I expect you to be very discreet about Mr. Elliott and his properties."

"The Rose Red Rapist?" Brian Elliott ignored the same barrier Adam had crossed and joined them. "Is that what this is about? Do you think he's been in my building?"

"We don't know that, Mr. Elliott." Annie tried to reassure him. "Right now, all we're investigating is a break-in."

"Then why doesn't *he* investigate it?" He pointed to Raj, then turned to face him. "You're not part of this task force, are you?"

"No, sir." Raj's caterpillar brows lifted in uneasiness at being put on the spot. "Dispatch said we had an entire warehouse to go through. There may be more of us coming from the lab."

"More?" The building's owner pointed to the far wall. "It's one stinking window, not a major crime!"

Raj cowered uncomfortably at the outburst and pulled out his cell phone. "I'll call and find out what's going on."

"Do that."

Regina tapped her watch. "Mr. Elliott, your three o'clock?"

Brian Elliott pulled a roll of antacids from his pocket and popped one into his mouth. "Make this go away, Adam. This will ruin me. I'll never sell another square foot of property if investors think that monster is…here."

Annie tried again. "Just because we're here doesn't mean we're investigating a rape."

Adam's gaze softened a moment for her. "Have you been reassigned since your assault?"

"No, but—"

"Then you *are* investigating on behalf of the task force."

"Who all has access to your building, Mr. Elliott?" Nick took charge of the questioning.

He waved his assistant forward. Annie put up her hands in protest. "Could we move this conversation to the other side of the room, away from the potential evidence?"

With a groan of impatience, Brian Elliott turned

and his staff followed. "Reggie, get the officer a list of architects, clients, inspectors—anyone who's been in here besides the three of us."

"Brian, there are confidentiality issues with prospective investors," Regina advised.

Adam squared off against Nick when they reached the top of the stairs. "You'll need a court order for a complete list, Detective."

"We'll get one." Nick offered the assurance like it was a challenge and turned back to the dark-haired owner. "How many old buildings like this do you own, Mr. Elliott?"

"I own four entire blocks in this neighborhood. I bought blighted property, so this isn't the first break-in we've had. But it is the first time a task force has shown up."

"Don't you also own the building where the Fairy Tale Bridal Shop is located?" Nick asked.

"Yes." His skin went pale beneath his tan. "That's where one of the rapist's first victims was abducted, isn't it?"

"And the Robin's Nest Floral Shop?" Where another victim had been taken.

"The owners are both business partners of mine." He reached for another antacid. "Oh, God, you think the rapes happened here? Is this a conspiracy against me? Is someone trying to ruin me? There are millions of dollars at stake here if people abandon this neighborhood."

Adam patted his boss's shoulder. "Relax, Brian.

There's nothing to link your name or your business to those assaults. Certainly nothing that's public knowledge." He dared Nick to deny it. "Is there, Detective? My client isn't under investigation, is he?"

"No." Nick closed his notebook and tucked it inside his jacket. "But my gut tells me there's some sort of connection between those attacks and these buildings."

"Your gut?" Adam laughed and gestured to the stairs for his boss and Regina Hollister to head back down. "You can't take your gut to court, Detective Fensom. Annie, I thought you had more class than to partner up with a banty rooster like this. He's all hot air and posturing. Pure speculation."

"I trust his gut a lot more than I trust your fancy words."

"Still thinking small, aren't you, dear? If there is one smirch against Mr. Elliott's reputation, one leak to the press that in any way infringes on his ability to conduct business, I will sue you both for harassment and slander."

She could see why a woman might be attracted to Adam—he was handsome, accomplished, good at his job. She logically understood why her craving for security and predictability would lead her to *think* he was the man for her. But she couldn't *feel* it. She suddenly understood that she'd been struggling with humiliation and loneliness this past year without him—not heartbreak. She wasn't feeling any attraction to Adam anymore. Not one little pang. Curious. She glanced over to Nick, who was waiting impatiently for Adam to stop talking his lawyerese, and her stomach did a little flip-flop. Her heart beat a little faster. Her skin tingled with some unnamed anticipation. Very curious.

"We're done here." Adam finished his speech.

Nick turned to catch her staring at him. The corner of his mouth crooked up in a questioning grin. "What?"

Oh, no. That couldn't be. Where was the logic in thinking she'd fallen in love with Nick?

"I need to process…this scene." She needed to process a lot more, but feeling the heat creeping into her cheeks, she turned away and pointed to the gathering of onlookers at the top of the stairs. "Without all this audience to distract me or touch something that might be evidence."

Nick's eyes gaze pinpointed the emotions painting her face, but thankfully he made no comment. "Okay. I'll take them downstairs to ask some more questions. You want me to get rid of Kapoor, too?"

She shook her head. "I'll put him to work."

"All right. Remember, I'm in the building. Just a phone call away."

She pushed him on his way. "I'll be fine. I'm on a closed-off floor. That window is the only way in here that's not secured."

She could still read the unasked questions in his eyes. "I'll post the officers at the bottom of the fire escape. I'll call you in an hour or so to check on you. Sooner if I get the interviews done."

That sounded good to her. But she was ready to work. She needed to work so she could sort through the recent discoveries she'd made. She turned him toward the others and gave him a gentle push. "Go."

Unable to erase the smile on her face at his reluctance to leave her, Annie set to work, gathering what she needed from her kit.

Her Indian friend from the lab was still waiting for some kind of direction. "What do you want me to do?" Raj asked.

"Why don't you go back to the fourth floor and talk to the men there. Find out who the foreman is and who first discovered the break-in, and if anyone got a look at the intruder so we can track him down. It wouldn't hurt to get elimination prints from the workers in case I find some up here."

"Understood." His phone rang and he pulled the cell from his pocket. He looked at the number and groaned before answering. "Hello. Now? Give me a sec, okay? I'm working. I will take care of it, I promise."

"If you need to take that, go ahead."

"Hold on." He pulled the phone from his ear. Frustration lined his dark skin. "Are you sure you don't want me to help up here? I can move the heavy things."

"I can manage. Go on. That sounds important."

"All right. Holler if you need something."

"I will. Thanks."

He put the phone back to his ear as he slipped behind the plastic. "I'm back. Yes. Too large." His voice faded as he headed down the stairs. "I can cover that."

Odd. Raj had gotten upset over a call about covering something large? Was he remodeling a room at home? Talking about paying a bill? Too large? Or *two* large?

Had her friend just placed a bet?

"I really don't know you outside of work, do I?" Instead of pondering the mysteries of Raj Kapoor, Annie turned her mental energy to the job at hand and went to work.

She relished the quiet as she moved methodically from one task to the next. She took pictures, dusted the space heater and window for prints, and studied the mattress and rolled-up plastic beside it with her ultraviolet light.

While she jotted notes and bagged samples, her brain cells kicked into overdrive as she immersed herself in the scene. But it wasn't the evidence in the room that took her focus, it was the observations about herself and the people who'd just left that demanded her attention.

After the initial shock of seeing her ex-fiancé at the crime scene had worn off, Annie realized she'd been grinning at Nick's inside joke about being called an odd duck rather than smiling to learn that Adam could still be concerned about her welfare.

Something about the cookie-cutter image Adam shared with Brian Elliott and his assistant Regina made her think she'd dodged a very boring bullet in the relationship department. Funny how a year apart—or maybe just a couple of life-changing days spent with someone so completely spontaneous and compassionate and full of life—could alter her feelings for the man.

She didn't crave predictability. She craved challenges and passion. She didn't need order. She needed someone who understood how disorderly her world could be. She didn't want someone to rescue her from the loneliness of her life. She wanted to grab hold of someone whose big family and bigger heart already made her feel included and important and happy to be exactly who she needed to be.

The facts were starting to add up.

"Nick Fensom, what have you done to me?" she whispered out loud. Now if she could only deduce whether Nick was feeling something more than friendship or a latent sexual attraction for her— and whether this closeness she felt between them would end once he decided he didn't need to play bodyguard for her anymore.

On that sobering thought, Annie stowed the last sample in her kit, and set her camera down beside it on the giant wooden spool she'd been using as a table. There wasn't much more she could do until she got the evidence to the lab to run the prints through AEFIS and identify the hairs and substances she'd collected. Still, she turned a slow three-sixty, surveying the room one last time for anything she'd missed.

"Like that." Although covered with a slight layer of dust kicked up from the construction work below, a faint line of shoe prints crossed from the trash heap over to the abandoned freight elevator. With all the traffic in here earlier, she'd discounted other shoe prints she'd found as being unusable. But this was a single set, untrammeled and uncontaminated beyond the heap of old junk.

Walking beside the prints so as not to disturb them, she followed the trail across the room. They stopped at the doorway in the deteriorating wall. Adjusting her flashlight, she stooped down and examined the doorknob. The old iron plate was hanging by a single screw and showed several gouges in the wood around it. She twisted the knob and discovered that it slipped back and forth inside the mechanism and didn't engage the lock. There was more evidence of tampering with the door frame. Even though there were slats broken and missing in the wall surrounding the elevator, if the intruder had come in here at night without a light, he might easily have mistaken the squared-off space as a room—someplace even warmer and more secure than the empty loft around it.

Annie angled her light down to the half shoe print that cut off beneath the closed door and wondered. Had the intruder gotten that door open? If so, had he discovered a broken elevator or empty shaft and fallen in? Her heart rate kicked up a notch at the dreadful possibility. She breathed in a little more deeply, her nose not detecting that distinct odor of death. Maybe he'd realized what it was and had gone back to the mattress to sleep. Or maybe he'd gone exploring after he'd slept and had fallen in.

If there was a body down there, if the man had hurt himself, maybe knocked himself unconscious, then he'd need immediate help. Annie straightened. "Hello?"

Maybe there was no one there. Maybe the intruder was safely back on his corner of the street and she was just imagining the worst because she'd seen so much death and pain these past few days that a simple broken window could never be answer enough.

"Hello?" she called louder, knocking on the wood. "Is anybody in there? Hello?"

For two seconds, she considered calling Nick. But her phone was back in her purse on the spool. If someone really was hurt in there, he'd need immediate attention. And if no one was there, why put Nick on alert and give him something unnecessary to worry about when he already had so much he felt responsible for?

With the knob broken, it took a couple tries to find the right leverage to pry the catch loose and pull the door open. "Hello?"

Annie swung it wide open and followed that last

shoe print to the lip of the old shaft. She aimed her light down about six feet to the roof of the black iron cage. Suspended by thick, rusting cables and coated with years of dust and decay, the elevator looked as though it had been frozen in time between floors.

It was filthy. It was dark. It showed evidence of rats or mice nesting there. But thankfully, there was no body.

She breathed out an embarrassed sigh and chided herself out loud. "Since when did you develop an imagination? Stick to what you do best—"

A pair of hands shoved her from behind. Annie screamed and flew over the edge, crashing down into the darkness below.

She landed hard on her feet, jarring every bone in her body, and pitched forward, hitting the cable and shaking the entire cage before sprawling across the elevator's metal roof. Her flashlight skittered over the edge and fell into the shaft below, plunging her into blackness.

Her head spinning, her cut throbbing, she got her hands beneath her and pushed her face away from the mucky layers of dirt and dampness, struggling to orient herself in the dark.

And then she heard the voice, whispered and vile, from above. "You should have quit while you were alive, Annabelle."

"No!" She tried to spin around, lift her head, see her attacker.

But he closed the door and walked away, sealing her in with her newfound imagination.

ANNIE'S PHONE RANG. And rang. And rang again.

Nick tapped his fingers against his thigh, waiting for the elevator to reach the lobby, after letting two guys in hard hats with a large box and a dolly take it up before him. Brian Elliott and Regina Hollister had left almost as soon as they'd reached the lobby, promising a meeting if he had any more questions. Adam Matuszak had stonewalled giving him any useful answers, then had excused himself with an accusatory glare when the site foreman came down to tell him the "Indian cop" wanted to take everyone's fingerprints. Nick had resigned himself to interviewing the workmen. Most of them had been on site since early that morning. None of them had seen a homeless man inside the building, although a few reported that there was a group who liked to gather at the corner sidewalk where the crew had left a steel drum and donated scrap lumber for the group to burn and have heat throughout the day during this icy-cold stretch of weather.

The detective in him wanted to follow up by interviewing the homeless men himself, but he wasn't going to leave Annie. Once she was done upstairs, they could both go talk to the men.

He idly wondered what piece of evidence had absorbed her attention now and how long it would take her to realize that her phone was ringing. Then she'd have to check her pockets and discover that she'd left her cell in her purse. And then she'd have to find her purse. The impulse to grin at her adorably eccentric obsession about her work was tempered by the sound of her voice mail message coming on. "Damn it, Annie."

Nick made a quick decision to take the stairs instead. It hadn't been an hour yet that they'd been out of contact, but he had a feeling it had already been too long.

He charged up the stairs. He knew the woman could get lost in her work and miss things, but he said he'd call. She should have answered.

Unless she couldn't answer.

"Ah, hell." Nick pushed through the next sheet of plastic and lengthened his stride to take the stairs two at a time. The second and third floors passed by in a blur. The fourth floor was still a hive of activity. Raj Kapoor was there. But no petite brunette.

Ignoring them all, Nick raced up the last flight and broke through the yellow crime scene tape at the top. "Annie!"

The emptiness registered first. Then hot-pink paisley drew his eyes to the window across the open room. There was her purse, her camera, her kit. But where was Annie?

And then he heard the pounding, metallic at first. He heard a thump against wood and swung his gaze around to the sound. "Annie!"

"Nick? Nick!" Her voice sounded muffled, distant but strong.

"Where are you?"

"I'm in here. In the old elevator."

He dashed to the broken-down walls at the end of the room. "Annie!" He tugged on the doorknob, but the whole thing—knobs, bolts, plate—came off in his hand. He swore and tossed the mechanism aside. He ran his hands around the frame, trying to find a spot to wedge his fingers inside. "Are you hurt?"

"The door's jammed. I can't reach it."

"Are you hurt?" he repeated. Then his eyes landed on the discarded knob assembly. "Hold on."

"Nick?"

"I'm coming, baby." He tore apart the rusted pieces. "Tell me if you're hurt."

"Just some bruises. The elevator is parked between floors and I'm on the roof. But it's gross down here. Mold, I think. I think something was living down here. And it's dark and..."

A fist squeezed around Nick's heart at the despair he heard in her voice. He picked up the long steel lynchpin and prayed years of neglect wouldn't let it bend or snap in two.

"And what?" he asked as he jammed the makeshift mini-crowbar between the door and frame and shoved as hard as he could. The wood around the lock plate splintered. With a twist and a jerk, he popped the door open and whipped it out of his way. "Annie?"

The meager light shone down on a grimy, squinting beauty, holding the remnants of a shredded CSI vest and clutching a broken chunk of wood. "If I was taller, I could have climbed out. I tried."

"I know you did, slugger." Lying down on his stomach, Nick reached past the vest she'd hooked on a bolt to try to pull herself up. "Give me your hand."

Mindful to check his relief until he knew she was all right, Nick waited for her to wipe off her hands and then stretch up on tiptoe. "I could have died because I'm so short. If you hadn't come looking for me…"

"You didn't answer your phone, so I came lookin'. You're not dying today. Not on my watch. Come on." Nick clasped his hand tightly around her wrist and pulled her up.

He grabbed a fistful of her coat and lifted her over the edge. Her chest fell across his and he rolled over with her, pulling her away from the opening. He cupped her dirt-streaked face, smoothed her hair away from the soiled bandage and checked the golden clarity in her beautiful eyes.

"I'm okay," she insisted, batting his hands away and trying to sit up.

"I'll be the judge of that. Now be still. You fell down a damn elevator shaft. What bruises? Where does it hurt?" He ran his hands along her arms and legs. Plenty of dirt, plenty of slime, but no broken bones, only a couple of ouches and quick catches of breath. "We need to get that bandage changed. Keep the wound clean."

"Let me up. I heard my phone ringing. I felt like an idiot for not having it on me so I could call for help."

"I said I'd be here."

"No." She planted her hands at the middle of his chest and shoved him back. "That's not all I heard. Now let me up."

"Fine." He wanted nothing more than to wrap her in his arms and carry her away from all this, and she didn't even want him touching her. He got up on his knees and swung the door shut before there were any more accidents. "Let's get out of here."

Annie was on her feet as soon as he was. "Wait. Don't move. Tell me exactly what you touched out here."

Nick picked up the pieces of the doorknob he'd used, waved them in front of her face and tossed them aside. "Thanks, Nick. I appreciate the rescue."

For a split second, her eyes locked on to his. And then she cupped his face between her hands and pulled herself up on tiptoe to press a kiss against his lips. And then another harder one. By the time the third kiss came, Nick had moved past shock and hurt, and was kissing her back. Fast. Sweet. Done.

She sank back onto her heels without releasing

him. Her eyes had warmed to that deep, soulful amber. "Thank you. I know you think I like to be alone all the time. But not really. And not like that." With a wry smile, she wiped a smudge off his jaw and pulled away. "The others left?"

"Yeah. Elliott and his assistant had a meeting. Matuszak skipped out somewhere. I don't think I made a very good impression on him. Raj is still on the fourth floor." The woman was complicated, but worth the patience it took to figure out when her brain and her emotions weren't always in sync. She was safe. They'd gotten to kisses three, four and five. He could slip back into detective mode, too. "Okay, I'm not understanding. How did you get stuck in there?"

"I didn't. Someone pushed me in." She walked a circle clear around him, scanning high, low, everywhere around the room. Nick's hands clenched into fists, damning the man who'd hurt her, damning himself for not sensing something was wrong sooner. "I could hear him out here. Messing with my crime scene."

He turned the same circle with her. *Check the emotional response,* he warned himself. Annie needed answers. He intended to give her whatever she needed. "I came up the stairs and made a beeline for the old elevator when I heard you. Used what I needed from the door. Didn't touch anything else."

She checked his work boots, then looked for a path that wasn't there. "That thorough son of a gun."

Even Nick could see what was missing. "He swept up. There's no dust between here and the stairs."

When she took off for the trash heap by the window, Nick figured it was safe to move and followed. She stopped beside the space heater and touched her fingers to the sooty carbon she'd left when she'd dusted for prints. "He didn't touch this." She moved on to the mattress and the window. "He didn't touch anything."

"Except you," Nick pointed out.

"Wait." She darted over to the wood spool where her purse sat beside her kit and camera. She opened her kit and pulled on a pair of sterile gloves. "He moved my camera."

"Why?" Nick crossed up beside her.

She inspected the camera from all angles before picking it up. "Hand me the magnifying glass out of my kit." Nick leaned in beside her and found the magnifier strapped to the lid with other tools. "I should dust it for prints. Although I expect he was wearing gloves." She held out her hand again. "Tweezers."

"Annie?" She pulled out the memory card, then pushed the camera into Nick's hands while she pulled out a small evidence envelope and dropped the computer chip inside. "What is it?"

"He switched the memory card in my camera."

"Who did?"

She pulled out a pen to mark the envelope. "I'm guessing a big man in a black parka? I didn't see him."

"The Cleaner?"

"Think about it, Nick. Nothing was taken in the break-in. The only thing damaged was that window. And if a homeless guy really did come in to spend the night, where's the evidence of that? Where did he go?" She repacked everything into her kit and peeled off the sterile gloves. "This crime scene isn't about the break-in or damaging Brian Elliott's renovation project."

"It's about you."

"It was a setup to get my camera. The photos from Rachel Dunbar's murder were still on it."

"It was a setup to leave you for dead."

She visibly shivered at the notion of what someone was willing to do to hide any evidence relating to the Rose Red Rapist. Nick set the camera on top of her kit and pulled her into his arms. His fingers found their way into the soft curls at her nape as she hugged her arms around his waist. "How did The Cleaner know I'd be assigned to this crime scene?"

"The location. It fits the witness testimony about being abducted and taken to a construction site where the actual rape occurred. It's in the right neighborhood where all the attacks have happened. He knew the task force would flag it."

"But we never made that detail about the attacks

public." The shivering stopped. "If The Cleaner knows those details…"

"…then he knows who our rapist is. He's not a fan."

"He's working with him."

Reluctantly, Nick released her to pull out his phone to call Spencer. "We need to tell the others. We need to dig a little deeper and find out who reported the break-in."

Annie slung her purse over her shoulder and gathered her things. "You need to take me to the lab to process this memory card."

Nick wrinkled up his nose and brushed a patch of moldy grit off her face. "I think I'd better take you home first."

Chapter Eleven

Annie unplugged the hair dryer and wound the cord around the handle in evenly spaced loops before putting it away in the bathroom drawer. She looked into the mirror over the sink to replace the gauze bandage on her forehead and run her fingers through her dampish curls, wondering how much longer she could hide out in the bathroom before Nick sent in a search party.

It wasn't like she didn't have a legitimate excuse for staying here, away from the laughter and home-cooked smells coming from her kitchen and living room. She'd literally soaped up twice to get rid of the dirt and what she suspected might be mouse droppings that had clung to her skin and clothes after her tumble down the old elevator shaft. She was truly grateful that the women in Nick's family cared enough to bring over soup and fresh bread and a hand-knit gift. Connie, Trudy, Natalie, Nadine and Nell were friendly and generous, and certainly loved to talk. But Annie wasn't quite sure how she fit in with her apartment full of guests.

Was she Nick's friend? Their friend? A lonesome charity case they'd adopted for the holidays? And just how was she supposed to get a word in edge-wise when there seemed to be a dozen conversations going on at any one time? What exactly was she supposed to contribute to the well-oiled Fensom machine that would show her gratitude and not make them regret their kindness to her in the first place?

Nick had said it was just what families did for each other.

But she wasn't family. She hadn't been part of a family—part of anything—for a long time.

And while she'd very much like to be a part of something like that again, right now she was just the odd duck their precious Nicky worked with.

Her reflection seemed to chide her shyness when it came to interacting with so many people all at once. She needed to suck it up and get dressed and get out there with her guests to eat some soup and thank them kindly and get over to the crime lab with the evidence she'd locked up in the back of Nick's Jeep.

She could figure out all the other answers later, after her job tonight was done.

Pulling her robe off the door hook, Annie slipped it on over her underwear and hurried down the hallway to her bedroom.

But she found a visitor there, as well. Nell Fensom sat cross-legged in the middle of Annie's bed, cradling a mysteriously attentive G.B. in her lap.

"I hope this is okay. I promise I didn't mess with anything." Nell stroked a line between G.B.'s dark ears, eliciting a purr that filled the room. "He seems to like it back here where it's quiet. But if you want me to leave, I'll go."

Annie looked from her Siamese cat's drowsy eyes to the petulant expression on the teenager's face, and closed the door. She'd had college roommates see her get dressed before. "You can stay." She put on a pair of argyle socks and pulled a pair of clean blue jeans off a hanger. "G.B. doesn't make friends easily. He must like you to let you pet him like that."

"I like him, too." Nell scooted to the edge of the bed and G.B. rode along in her lap without changing his tune. "It's just, if one more person asks me how I'm feeling…"

"How you're feeling about what?" Annie zipped her jeans and opened her dresser to find a long-sleeved T-shirt and a sweater.

"I broke up with Jordan. I thought about what you said this morning, that he was just using me." Nell pulled out her phone and showed Annie the screen. "I sent him a text."

Annie read as Nell scrolled through it. Not very concise, but the meaning was clear.

She pulled the T-shirt over her head and reached for the blue sweater. "Looks to me like you handled it just fine. How did he take it? Did he give you an answer?"

Nell cradled the cat in one arm to stand and hand Annie her phone. "A few times. He's mad, but it's not like I'm going to change my mind." She pulled up her sleeve beneath the draped cat to reveal the angry bruise encircling her wrist. "I know the kind of people Nick used to work with. This is nothing compared to what some of them do. Maybe I was trying to get my family's attention. I mean, Jordan's cute and stuff, but—"

"A few times?" As disturbing as the abusive mark on Nell's arm was, the sheer number of texts on the girl's phone frightened Annie even more.

Still luv u. Want u back.

I won't take no 4 an ansr.

WTF! Talk to me.

U R MINE.

Annie skipped her shoes and new pink scarf and opened the door. "Nick?" She opened the door and hurried down the hallway, interrupting him at the kitchen counter with a spoonful of minestrone half-way to his mouth. "Look at these. All from Garza. I'll bet there's a hundred of them."

Nick wiped his mouth with a napkin as he scrolled through the text messages. "Son of a bitch."

"Annie?" Nell had dumped the cat and run through the apartment after her. "What are you doing? I showed you that stuff in confidence."

"Nell, this is not something you keep secret. This

is harassment." She looked straight into the girl's stricken blue eyes. "First he hurts you and now he's threatening you? Trying to coerce you into taking him back?"

"He just feels bad. I text my friends when I'm upset." She tried to snatch her phone back from her brother, but Nick held it high over his head, easily out of her reach.

At the same time, he was on his own phone, calling the deputy commissioner of KCPD. "Uncle George. I need a twenty on Jordan Garza right now." Nell surrendered the fight, plopping down on the couch, her whole body in a pout. Nadine and Natalie flanked their sister on either side, offering unwanted condolences, while Connie fixed Annie a mug of soup and Trudy anxiously followed her son down the hallway, eavesdropping on his conversation. Nick was hugging his mom around the shoulders when they came back, the conversation over. "George is heading over to the house right now in case Garza shows up there. It'll be all right, Mom."

"I knew I didn't like that boy." Trudy patted Annie's arm as she circled around her to include Connie in the hugs. "To think he hurt my baby."

Connie reached over to squeeze Annie's hand. "Thank you."

"For what?"

Connie's delicate white brows arched in surprise. "Protecting our family."

It was on the tip of Annie's tongue to remind

her she'd just been doing her job, but another mini-drama was unfolding.

Nick circled around the back of the couch to give Nell's shoulder a reassuring squeeze. "I'll take care of it, Nellie. Everything will be fine."

The teenager shrugged him off and shot to her feet. She whirled around with tears in her eyes. "You said Jordan was a problem and I took care of it. I'm not a baby. You don't have to fix everything for me."

"No, you're a young woman, and I'm protecting you. I'm doing my job—as a cop and as your brother." She tipped her head to the ceiling and groaned. "I need the people I love to be safe. But I'd do the same for any woman who was being treated like this." When that got no response except a tear rolling down her cheek, Nick muttered a curse and headed back to the relative privacy of the hallway. "I'm calling Spencer and telling him I need someone to escort you all back home while I take Annie to the lab." He nodded to her as he stalked past. "Eat something and then we'll go."

Connie and Trudy busied themselves pouring soup for the women while they set places in front of the stools at the kitchen counter. A couple of silent minutes passed before Nell came over to Annie and quietly asked, "Is Nicky right? Is sending me all those texts against the law?"

"Yes, it's sexual harassment." Annie wasn't sure if the rest of the family knew the whole truth, but she wasn't going to lie. "And that bruise on your wrist is an assault."

"Oh, my God. Nellie." The other women gathered around in a protective circle, crying and hugging and bringing ice and drying tears.

Annie sat apart and watched. Nell was lucky she had someone like Nick looking out for her. Even if she wasn't sure she wanted him to.

Leaving that familiar-sounding revelation percolating in her mind, Annie carried her mug of soup to the front window and peeked through the sheers to the snowy twilight outside. It all looked peaceful, serene. Some of that serenity seemed to be finding its way into her cautious heart. Her apartment hadn't seen this many people, or this kind of emotional energy for years. And even though they were dealing with a difficult topic, it was nice to hear all the activity behind her.

That, however, wasn't so nice.

Just as Annie started to relax with the company in her tiny place, her pulse went on red alert. She needed Nick. Now.

"He's on his way." She nearly plowed into his chest as he reentered the living room. "Easy, slugger." With a deft grasp, he saved the minestrone from spilling down the front of his sweater and caught Annie by the arm. "What's wrong?"

He passed the cup off to one of his sisters as Annie pulled him to the window.

"Look out there." She pointed outside to where

a black Chevy Suburban was parked near the entrance to the lot across the street. "Is that the same car from last night?"

"Our friend, E-14." Nick closed the curtain, checked the gun on his belt and grabbed his jacket off the rack by the front door. "I'll go introduce myself."

Annie unhooked the locks while he zipped up. "Stay put?"

"What do you think?" He squeezed her hand and hurried down the stairs.

All the Fensom women lined up beside Annie at the window to watch Nick creeping swiftly over the snow, from tree to tree in the courtyard, to come up behind the black SUV. With night approaching, the streetlamps were on, but Annie could see Nick's point about too many dark places where someone could hide. If not for the tiny clouds of breath that followed him through the shadows, she'd have lost him completely.

But now she spotted him darting across the street to the opposite sidewalk. She caught her breath, wrinkling the curtain in her fist when she saw his gun drawn down at his side. "Be careful," she whispered.

"Amen," Connie whispered beside her.

"Jordan!" The front door swung open behind them and Nell ran down the stairs, shouting her ex-boyfriend's name. "Don't shoot him! Jordan!"

The black SUV belonged to Jordan Garza?

"Nell!" Annie caught the door and hurried down the stairs after her. "Call 9-1-1. Call Spencer Montgomery." She tossed the orders over her shoulder and burst out into the cold damp night after her. "Nell, get back here!"

"Jordan!"

Hearing his sister's warning shout, Nick gave up on stealth and ran straight to the driver's window with his gun leading the way. "KCPD! Get out of the car!"

"That's Ramon's car. Jordan's with him." Nell slowed down when she reached the slippery sidewalk, but Annie never broke stride.

She grabbed the teen and pulled her down into the snow behind a tree. "Get back here. It isn't safe." Nell tried to get free, but Annie threw her entire body weight on top of the girl to hold her there. "I've got her, Nick!"

"I don't want him to die."

"Which one?" Annie demanded to know. "You don't think your boyfriend's got a gun in there, too?"

Her words finally got through to the girl. She stared up at Annie from the crude snow angel their struggle had made. Her voice was quiet, sad. "I'm sorry."

The driver gunned the engine, shifted into gear.

"I said get out of the car!" Nick understood the situation now, too. "You're under arrest, Garza! You and Sanchez get on the ground now!"

The SUV's passenger window rolled down and Jordan Garza yelled across the street. "I gave you a chance to be with me, Nellie! You're screwed, baby! You're screwed! Punch it, Ramon!"

Sirens in the distance muffled his shouts.

"Get him, Nicky!" Nell's allegiance had suddenly changed.

The car hadn't been after Annie at all. The driver, a thug friend of Jordan, no doubt, had been following Nick, trying to keep tabs on whatever information they could get about KCPD's gang enforcement activities, probably never realizing that gangs were no longer his primary concern at the department.

The vehicle's big tires squealed for traction on the icy street.

"Don't do it, Sanchez!" The SUV peeled away from the curb. Two shots rang out.

"Nick!" Annie raised her head.

He'd shot out a tire. The big vehicle fishtailed into the street, smashing into a couple of cars on the opposite side. The driver accelerated again, forcing the SUV to lurch forward.

Flashing lights bounced off the wall of the apartment buildings as an unmarked cruiser whipped around the corner, blocking their escape. It screeched to a stop and Spencer Montgomery jumped out, bracing his gun on the open door of the car and ordering them to stop.

Ramon Sanchez shifted his souped-up Chevy into Reverse and barreled back past the courtyard until *bam!*—a black-and-white KCPD truck blocked the street behind them and they crashed into another car. With Detective Montgomery coming straight down the middle of the street with his gun pointed at the windshield and Nick running toward them from the side, the two 7th Streeters threw open their doors and jumped out of the SUV, running for the only open ground in sight—the snowy courtyard where Annie and Nell crouched beneath an evergreen tree.

Big Pike Taylor climbed out of the black-and-white truck and opened the door behind him. "Get down on the ground! Now!"

But the boys kept running.

"No guns!" Nick shouted. "We've got civilians!"

"This is my fault," Nell moaned.

"Just stay down," Annie warned, pushing her back into the snow.

Sanchez flew past, heading for the break between the buildings. Jordan ran by them. A flash of denim and brown leather pounded through the snow after him. A terrible, wild bark filled the night.

"Hans, get him!"

In a matter of seconds, Nick had tackled Jordan Garza and had him in handcuffs. Pike's K-9 partner, Hans, had Ramon Sanchez by the arm on the ground, pleading for mercy and a quick arrest.

Annie didn't let Nell up until both teens had been loaded in the back of a black-and-white police car that had answered the 9-1-1 call. Pike was playing a rewarding came of tug-of-war with his German shepherd. She and Nell were both wet and shivering when Nick ran over to find them. "You two okay?"

Nell launched herself into her big brother's arms and hugged him tight around the neck. "I'm sorry, Nick. I'm so sorry. I wasn't thinking. I just wanted Jordan to go away—I didn't want him to get hurt. But he's such a tool."

Nick hugged her just as tight, teasing her the way a proper big brother should. "Yeah, you could have been with that."

Nell smacked him in the shoulder and pulled away as Spencer Montgomery walked up. "One mystery solved," he said. "I'll bet my next paycheck that parts, if not all, of that SUV have been stolen. Plus, we can book them on harassment charges and evading arrest." He glanced at Annie and then at Nick. "You two ready to go back to work?"

Annie's teeth were chattering. "Yes, sir."

Nick took off his jacket and draped it around Nell's shoulders before wrapping his arm around Annie and snugging her close to his side, warming them both. He glanced up to the four women standing in the upstairs window, their faces now wreathed in smiles. "You'll take care of the situation here?"

Spencer leaned in. "Did Connie cook?"

Nick grinned. "Homemade bread and minestrone soup."

"Oh, yeah." Annie had never seen the task force

leader smile like that before. "For the price of one dinner, I'll make sure your family gets safely home."

"Thanks, buddy." Nick turned Annie toward the building's front door. "Change your clothes and let's get over to the lab. I want to find out who The Cleaner is. I'm running out of patience trying to ID the guy who's doing all he can to keep us from solving this case."

"You? Running out of patience?" Annie laughed when Spencer and Nell both echoed the same thing she'd been thinking.

The laughter stopped abruptly when she remembered that she'd run down the stairs without stopping to get her coat, her purse or a key card. "I can't get back in. We'll have to ring the buzzer and hope your mom or—"

But the door opened for them and Roy Carvello stepped out on the porch. How long had he been standing there watching them? "Good evening, Officers. Annie, I see we've had a little trouble. Is there anything I can do to help?" He reached for Nell's hand and winked. "How about you, miss? Can I help you inside where it's toasty warm?"

Nick stepped up to hold the door, and nudged Roy back onto the landing. "Dude, hitting on my sister? Seriously?"

For a moment, Annie thought she saw something blaze hotly in Roy's brown eyes. But it was gone as quickly as she'd imagined it. He smiled and moved aside, letting them move up the stairs ahead of them.

There was something about brown eyes Annie needed to remember.

But right now, Nick's arm was around her. She was surrounded by friends and joining a family she was growing fonder of by the minute.

For the first time in forever, it seemed, she didn't feel alone.

SATISFIED THAT THE FIRST-FLOOR locker rooms were as deserted as the rest of the crime lab building was at this time of night, Nick turned out the lights and headed to the last place he hadn't checked, the staff cafeteria. Wide-open and empty, save for tables and chairs. Kitchen door locked. Adjoining restrooms empty. From the morgue in the basement to the executive offices on the fifth floor, every passageway and door in the lab building was either empty or locked up tight.

He should be able to relax his vigil, right? But his warning instincts were creeping up the chart of *too good to be true.*

As much as he hated to leave Annie on her own in the third-floor lab, he'd made the sweep to try to settle that niggling twist in his gut that the building, and Annie, weren't as secure as he'd like them to be. She'd insisted the whole place would be empty this time of night, especially with the holidays. And other than the guard who'd checked them in at the front security desk, he hadn't run across another soul inside.

Of course, he'd been off his game for a few days now. But Jordan Garza was in a jail cell, out of his sister's life—eliminating one giant distraction. He and Annie had made a breakthrough on the task force's investigation, determining that there were two perps—the Rose Red Rapist and The Cleaner—and that the accomplice who'd done such a thorough job of compromising the task force's evidence thus far, along with some hired help, knew the rapist's identity. There'd been too many similarities between that break-in at Brian Elliott's textile warehouse and the surviving victim accounts of the crime scene where they'd been assaulted to attribute them to coincidence. Knowing that doubled their opportunity to catch this guy—there might not be a living witness who could identify the rapist, but there was an accomplice out there who could. Thanks to Annie's tenacity and eye for detail, they were finally moving forward again in their investigation.

And then there was Annie herself. Sweet, tempting Annie Hermann—a thorn in his side, an itch he couldn't quite reach. She was unlike any woman he'd ever known. Complicated. Klutzy. Sometimes so unsure of herself and sometimes so brave. A touch from her could center his world or tilt it on its axis. She was smart. Funny. Unpredictable. Passionate about her work, about finding the truth, about making the people and the world around her better.

But were those glimpses of passion she'd shared with him a sign of what could be between them? Did he have the patience to wait for her to learn to trust in what they could be together? Was he being too impulsive and foolish and eager to think that together they could be pretty damn good?

He should stick to the instincts that had served him so well up until that night in the alley. He should stick to his job the way Annie was so devoted to hers, and stop letting all those jumbled-up thoughts distract him from that crawling sense of unease that told him there was danger lurking in the shadows.

Something was off with this setup tonight. Empty building. Alarms activated. The parking lot was empty except for Nick's Jeep, a pair of vehicles belonging to the security guards at the parking lot entrance and inside the building, and a couple more cars that looked like they'd been parked there for some time, judging by the snow piled around their tires.

Maybe it was that run-in with Garza that had put him on edge like this. He'd seen the gun on the seat between Garza and Sanchez. He'd heard his sister running out across open ground, had watched Annie charge right out of the building after her. He could have lost so much tonight.

It didn't matter what Annie might or might not

feel for him. He wasn't going to risk losing anyone else.

That left one last place to secure.

Nick shrugged into his jacket and pulled out his cell phone and punched in Annie's number. Exchanging a nod with the security guard who'd checked them in a half hour earlier, Nick strolled through the lobby to the ultramodern glass-and-steel wall that created the building's two-story facade.

"Good night," the guard called to him. "Have a good one."

"I'll be back in a few minutes," Nick promised him. "Miss Hermann's still here."

"The doors lock automatically after hours. You'll need a key card to get back in, Detective."

"I'll knock."

Annie picked up on the second ring and Nick grinned on his way out the door. "Yes, I'm still here. You know, if you keep calling me every five minutes, I'll never get this done and we'll be here all night."

"Just wanted to make sure you still have your phone on you, and it's not twenty-feet away in your purse where it does you no good if you can't get to it."

"I'm keeping it right here in the pocket of my lab coat."

"Don't set it down on the table and forget about it when I hang up."

She laughed, and Nick wondered if he'd ever get tired of hearing that rare sound. "I won't. Where are you now?"

"Walking around the perimeter outside. I want to double check that all the access points are secure. I'll chat with the guard in the parking lot, too, to see if anyone else has shown up since we went in." He tipped his face up toward the starry sky and inhaled a calming breath when he saw the bright light from the third-story window bank pouring through the glass into the night. "I can see you from here." Besides the guard's desk in the center of the lobby, every other floor was dark, reassuring Nick that she was safe up in her lab, sorting through the evidence she'd gathered from Brian Elliott's textile warehouse while she waited for the results of a computer search through AEFIS to find a match for the thumbprint she'd found on the swapped-out memory card in her camera. "Well, I can at least see the lights from your lab."

"Is this better?" She came to the window and waved.

Nick flipped her a salute. "If I was a sniper, it'd be perfect. Now keep your door locked and get back to work. Don't go anywhere else without telling me. I'll be back up there in ten."

She moved away from the window, disappearing from sight. "I'll be here."

He was counting on it.

Clipping his phone back on his belt, Nick zipped

his jacket, pulled his scarf more tightly around his neck and stepped off into the snow. Just like the guard had indicated, every door Nick tried was locked up for the night, from the emergency exits to the service entrance in the back to the three garage doors where the M.E.'s wagon pulls in to drop off a body or entire vehicles that needed to be processed were stored.

Everything was perfectly secure, inside and out. Too perfect.

The blast of damp, single-digit air revived his senses after another long day. Why couldn't he see what was wrong here? The lights were still on in Annie's lab. The two guards were on duty. The number of vehicles in the lot was still the same. He scrubbed his gloved hand over the scruff of his beard and surveyed the parking lot itself, scanning every landscape bush, every inch of asphalt, every lamppost and car.

And then the hazy dysfunction he'd been stuck in for nearly three days now cleared away and he saw it.

That was the thing that didn't fit.

The guard sitting in the parking lot kiosk had changed the color of his hair.

Trusting his instincts in a way he hadn't for seventy-two hours, Nick put in a call to Spencer, requesting backup for the second time that night.

"Based on what?" his partner asked.

"My gut is twisted in a knot."

"I'm on my way."

Nick jogged across the lot, approaching the guard's kiosk from the guy's blind side. Pasting a friendly grin on his face, Nick rapped on the glass, startling the guard to his feet.

With a cautionary hand on his sidearm, the guard slid open the kiosk door. His gaze dropped to the badge hanging around Nick's neck. "Yes, Officer?"

"Where's the other guy?" Nick asked. "The one who checked me in earlier?"

The guard's posture relaxed a fraction. "Shift changed at ten."

"Let me see your ID." Nick turned away, nodding to the cars in the lot. None of them had moved. "Is the guard you relieved still here?"

"He went inside to change into his civvies."

Nick was ready when he caught the flash of movement out of the corner of his eye. The guard had pulled his weapon and raised it above Nick's head, swinging it down like a club.

Nick lurched to the side, letting the man's momentum throw him off balance, giving Nick the opportunity to get behind him and knock him to the pavement. He stomped on the man's hand and kicked the gun away. In a matter of seconds, Nick had a choke hold around the fake guard's neck. He squeezed tighter and tighter until the man passed out and went limp in his arms. Nick dropped him to the ground and stepped over him to retrieve the gun and stuff it into the back of his belt.

"It's a gun, idiot," he chided his unconscious attacker. "Not a baseball bat. You shoot it."

After a glance around to make sure no one had seen that little scuffle and sounded the alarm, Nick dragged him back inside the kiosk where he discovered the original guard lying on the floor. Bleeding from a gash at his temple, he, too, was unconscious, and had been bound and gagged with duct tape.

Nick immediately bent down to check his pulse. Weak but steady. He cut the injured guard loose, then checked his pockets. His key card and ID badge were gone, but he had a pair of handcuffs on him that Nick used to secure his attacker. He pulled the tape off the guard's mouth and put it on his attacker. Then Nick pushed to his feet, pulled out his phone and called Spencer right back, warning him to include an ambulance and all the friends he wanted to invite to the party.

If the armed men guarding the place had been taken out, then there was probably a team of intruders trying to get into the lab. No. Probably already in the lab because there'd been no visible signs of forced entry. With the fallen guard's key card, they'd have free access to most of the building.

Nick was damn well going to make his own access now.

Instead of wasting his time on locked doors, and unsure whether the guard inside had been compromised, as well, Nick ran straight to his Jeep. He cranked the engine, released the brake, shifted into gear and jammed the pedal to the floor. Taking a cue from the gangbangers who'd torn up Annie's neighborhood earlier, he barreled toward the front entrance, taking aim at all that glass. The Jeep jumped the curb and rammed the front doors, shattering glass and steel and screeching to a stop in the middle of the lobby.

Glass rained down. Security lights flashed. Alarms blared.

Nick shed his coat and pulled it over his head, protecting himself from the falling debris as he kicked open the door and climbed out.

His first check was the front desk. Empty.

Had the guard there been taken out, too? Had he, like Nick, sensed the danger inside the walls and left his post to check it out? Unlike the guard out front, the man he'd talked to inside was the same man he and Annie had talked to earlier. She seemed to know him. His ID had checked out.

Nick's phone rang right on cue. "Annie?"

"What the hell is going on? Are you all right?"

He dropped his jacket, shed his gloves and pulled his Glock. "Where are you?" he asked, heading for the stairwell, heading for her.

"My lab."

"Kill the lights and hide somewhere. Turn your phone to silent. We've got intruders.

"I think The Cleaner is here."

Chapter Twelve

Intruders?

Annie switched her phone to silent mode and watched the images on the computer screen cycle by with a new print and a new *No Match* message changing with every millisecond. Ticking off the time like the sense of impending danger closing in around her.

They were so close to identifying the man who could break the Rose Red Rapist case wide open.

She was so close to another attempt to kill her again. To stop her from finding out the truth.

Truth? Death?

The answer was simple.

Annie ran to the switches by the door and turned off all the lights. The light from the computer screen blazed like a spotlight in the darkness and she zigzagged back through the stainless-steel tables to her work station. She spared a second to save the search before shutting down the system and plunging the room into darkness.

The only illumination was a greenish glow

from the security lights in the hallway, streaming through the glass wall that separated the main passage from the more sterile environs of each lab. Annie huddled beneath her workstation for endless seconds, waiting for Nick to reach her. The only sounds she heard were her own quick, tense breaths and the pounding of her pulse in her ears.

The pulse beat took on an even rhythm, and for a second, she marveled at her ability to calm herself. But her senses kicked in and she realized she was hearing the sound of stealthy footsteps in the hall.

"Nick," she breathed in relief, pulling her phone from her pocket and texting his name. *Is that you?*

She held her breath as the footsteps became a shadow. Then two shadows passing in front of the windows.

Annie pressed her hand to her mouth to stifle her frightened gasp. Black stocking masks. Black clothes. Tall. Dangerous.

She cleared the text and typed again. *They're here.*

She scanned the shadows, looking for something she could arm herself with. Rolling chairs. Big, high-tech machines. Heavy steel tables.

The chemical cabinet caught her eye and she darted from her hiding spot, crawling across the floor, keeping an eye on the shifting shadows. She could hear muffled voices now, words like "Not here" and "Find them." They were searching for something. Or someone.

Her? Nick? That lone fingerprint? Something else?

Her phone vibrated in her pocket and she jumped, knocking into a chair and sending it spinning. She caught the seat and stilled it instantly, dropping to the floor as far out of sight from the two in the hallway as she could get. The two figures outside paused. Had they heard that tiny noise?

Annie froze to the spot, ignoring the incoming message, until they moved to an office across the hall. She heard the beep of a key card being recognized as it swiped through the lock. They had access to the building, she realized with a disturbing eye for details. They weren't the explosive break-in she'd heard down below.

She checked the incoming text from Nick, feeling at once alarmed and relieved. *On my way. Trust no one but me.*

Impostors again. Fake cops. A man who was a mystery hiding in plain sight. Standing right outside the door to her lab.

Once the intruders disappeared inside the office, Annie jammed the phone into her jeans pocket and hastened to get across the room to the cabinet before they came back out. She sorted through a couple of bottles of possibilities before pulling out a potentially volatile mix. She grabbed a beaker and an extension cord before crawling across the lab to the tent oven that faced the door. If she got trapped in here, if anyone came through that door who wasn't Nick, she intended to make a way out for herself.

She held her breath, squinting against the toxic fumes as she poured the concoction together into the beaker. Stretching her neck to peer over the edge of the table she hid behind, Annie made sure the intruders were still across the hall before she reached up and placed the beaker inside the oven where they often used chemicals and heat to make a print appear on evidence. She set the time and temperature she wanted but unplugged the machine. Then she pulled the cord with her as she flattened herself and crawled underneath the next table. She plugged the extension into the power source, held the end of both cords in her hands and waited.

From her low vantage point she could see black booted feet coming out of the office across the hall. She made out a few more muffled phrases. "Split up." "Check progress." "Find that cop."

They were after Nick. Annie's blood dropped to the temperature of the cold tiles beneath her chest and stomach. If they hurt him…if he got killed trying to save her…

The emotions that welled up inside her were overwhelming. It felt like being caught up in that helpless wave of grief she'd gone through after her parents had died. But Annie was no teenager anymore. And she wasn't facing this adversary alone.

The emotions receded and clarity returned.

"Come and get me."

NICK STILLED HIS RAPID breathing after his sprint up the stairs. He eased his Glock into a comfortable grip between his hands, then released it with his left hand to push open the door to the third-floor hallway.

But footsteps pinging on the steel mesh stairs above him had him instantly switching tactics. He ducked into the blind corner of the landing and pressed his back against the concrete wall, giving himself the advantage of seeing who approached before he gave away his position.

Black shoes, darks pants, handgun pointed down, leading the way. Nick readied his own weapon. Tan shirt, badge on pocket.

He blew out a silent sigh of relief as he recognized the guard from the front desk. The gun came up as soon as he saw Nick.

"Whoa, buddy." Nick put up one hand and lowered his Glock. "It's me, Detective Fensom. Remember?"

"Yeah." The guard nodded, hurrying down the last few steps to join him. "Thank God. Have you found your girlfriend yet?"

"CSI Hermann's in her lab. I'm on my way to her now." Nick glanced up the stairwell and down, worrying about the sound of their conversation carrying to someone above them or below. "They got to your buddy in the parking lot. Any idea how many of them we're up against?"

"Yeah, at least one more."

"What floor?"

The guard's gaze darted to the number on the door. "Third."

"Hell." Too close to Annie. "Then let's split up. There's another set of stairs on the opposite—"

The guard raised his weapon and shot Nick before he had a chance to do more than see it coming. The bullet hit him in the left shoulder. His gun bounced down the stairs to the next landing and Nick tumbled down along with it. Every step was a bruised muscle or cracked rib until he hit the concrete floor and slammed to a stop against the wall.

Fire seared through his chest. His lungs ached. He rolled onto his back and let the pain clear his spinning head. He blinked the approaching man into focus and blindly reached around beside him to find his own weapon.

Another fake guard—and he'd been in the building with them this entire time. "If you hurt Annie…"

The smiling man came down the stairs one triumphant step at a time, pulling out his phone and punching in a number as he lined his gun up with Nick's head for the kill shot. "I got the guy," he reported to whoever answered. "Find the woman. He says she's in the third-floor lab. She's all yours now."

Nick grunted, pain exploding down his arm as he tried to scoot some distance between him and the barrel of the gun pointed between his eyes.

"Yes, ma'am."

The guard pocketed the phone ánd squeezed the trigger.

With a feral roar, Nick lashed out, dislocating the guy's kneecap with his elbow. The shot ricocheted off the wall, spewing out chips of concrete that clawed through his sweater as he kicked up his legs and rolled into the stunned man. With a twist of his hips, he took the man down hard, reversing positions so that Nick was now on top. He raised his fist to strike another blow, but the other guy had hit his head on one of the steel steps and was out cold.

Wincing in pain with every breath, Nick pulled his Glock from beneath his attacker's legs, tucked the second gun into his belt and kicked the guard's phone down the stairs where it shattered into pieces. Before he pulled himself back up those stairs, Nick bent over the guard's body. Instead of checking for a pulse, he pressed a thumb to one eyelid and forced it open.

"Green eyes."

The idiot out in the parking lot kiosk had blue eyes. That meant there was at least one more brown-eyed thug somewhere in the building tracking down Annie.

He secured his Glock in his fist and headed up to the third floor.

The bastard would have to get through Nick first.

"SHE'S IN HERE."

The shadow lurked outside her door.

Annie had heard a gunshot in the distance. But she couldn't think about that right now. If Nick had gotten hurt—or worse—then it was up to her now to survive and report and testify. She knew she'd make a great witness on the stand, once she dealt with these people who wanted to erase the truth she'd uncovered. A thumbprint from a crime scene. An accomplice's identity if she could only find the match. The key to arresting Rachel Dunbar's killer and getting him to reveal the identity of the Rose Red Rapist in exchange for a life sentence instead of a lethal injection.

But she had to stay alive first. And one of the intruders was right here, only a few feet from where she lay beneath the steel table.

"Take care of her. I'll find out how we're doing with the computer program. Almost all the data regarding the case in the lab's system has been erased. Without those pictures, that CSI has nothing she can pin on us. And if she's gone, then she can't even testify to what she saw in that alley. I silenced one witness for him. We'll silence this one, too." The voice giving the orders was higher pitched. A woman's voice. "He'll be very pleased."

Odd. Why would a woman have any inclination whatsoever to help a man like the Rose Red Rapist? The Cleaner was a woman?

The tall shadow passed by the windows and disappeared in the greenish light from the hallway. The opportunity to learn anything more about the ringleader of this late-night invasion had gone.

This fight was one-on-one now. Brains versus brawn.

Annie didn't wait to give Muscles a chance to hurt her again. As soon as the masked figure pushed open the door, she plugged in the two cords she held, connecting the current to the tent oven and baking the chemicals inside. One. Two.

Boom!

The explosion happened sooner than she'd expected. Annie curled into a ball beneath the protective steel, flinching as shrapnel from the oven and beaker and nearby appliances and glass shot across the room like hundreds of tiny, deadly missiles.

The floor shook when the man hit the floor without a moan, without a twitch.

As soon as the glass stopped falling, Annie scrambled out of her hiding place and crawled over to the gaping hole where the door and window beside it had been. The man lay in a sea of shattered debris, blood pooling beneath him. Ignoring the shock of what she'd just done, she looked past the dead man's plump belly and pulled off his stocking mask. She recoiled from the vaguely familiar face—blond hair, receding hairline—a match to the artist's sketch drawing of the man who'd impersonated Sergeant Steven Gobel on New Year's Eve.

So where was the man who'd attacked her in the alley? The man with the raspy, unidentifiable voice. The man with brown eyes who'd probably shoved her down that elevator shaft, too.

More desperate than ever to find Nick and help, Annie peeked into the hallway. Once she was sure it was empty, she got to her feet and ran to the elevator. She pushed the call button in a panic five times before remembering Nick's warning to stay put. But the other man would have heard the explosion by now and would be coming back.

Her first instinct was to run to the stairs. She put her hands on the exit door, but the sound of footsteps running up the other side had her backing away, spinning, searching for another place to hide.

The light peeking from the office door at the end of the hallway drew her like the promise of salvation. If one man was dead and the woman had left, then logic told her the room would be empty.

She dashed down the hallway, then stuttered to a halt as the door opened wider. Not empty. She tried to retreat. But the sleeve of a white lab coat had already appeared in the open doorway. A head of dark brown hair appeared next and someone peeked out in a glimpse as furtive and frightened as she had been when she'd emerged from hiding a few moments earlier.

"Annie?"

"Raj!" Her chest nearly collapsed in relief at the sight of a familiar face. "Get back in there. It's not safe."

"I heard an explosion. Is that guy—" his eyes slid across the hall to the fractured windows and damaged lab and man lying in the middle of it all "—dead?"

"Yes." She started forward again, urging Raj back into the safety of the office. "There are intruders in the building. A woman and some men. They said something about erasing data from our computers. We need to get inside where it's safe. Nick Fensom is here. Help is coming."

Instead of seeking safety, Raj took another step out of the office. His caterpillar brows had knit together. His brown eyes were crinkled with something like regret.

Notice the details, Annie. It was what she'd been trained to do.

Black shoes and pants beneath the white lab coat. He held a computer disk in one hand and a gun in the other.

Raj Kapoor had brown eyes. Just like the eyes in that alley.

He disguised the accent of his voice on a raspy whisper. "There's no help coming, Annabelle."

The stairwell opened behind her. "Annie!"

"Nick?" She whirled around to see the man she loved, his intense blue eyes and gun focused on the man behind her.

"Get down!"

Annie threw herself to the floor as a burst of gunfire erupted over her head. A heartbeat later, silence and the sulfuric smell of gunpowder filled the air.

"Annie?" She pushed herself to her feet as Nick ran to her. He was bruised and bleeding and solid and strong as he wrapped one arm around her and caught her tight against his chest. "Are you all right?" He lifted her up and set her on the floor behind him, brushing the hair away from her face. "Annie, are you all right?"

"I'm fine." She felt the sticky warmth of his blood beneath her hand and heard his oof of protest when she pushed away. "You're hurt. You've been shot."

She turned on the man she'd once called a friend.

"Raj, how could you?" But he was on the floor, bleeding out from two bullet holes in his chest. Annie knelt down beside him. "Oh, Raj."

"I'm sorry. She…made me. I owed so much… money." Every word was a dying gasp.

She felt Nick's hand on her shoulder. "It wasn't Kapoor. I found another fake cop in the stairwell."

"Raj!" His eyes were glazing over, his strength was fading. "Who was that woman? Who is she?"

He blinked her into focus one last time. "She knows…rapist. Protecting…"

Annie clasped his hand between hers. "I know who she's protecting. Why, Raj? Who is she?"

"She wants…"

"What?" Annie squeezed a little harder. "I know she killed Rachel Dunbar, Raj. What does she want?"

His voice feathered away into that raspy, haunting tone that had once frightened her. "I'm sorry… we all had to…help."

Raj's hand went slack in hers and he was gone.

"Come on." Nick's hand was beneath her elbow, pulling her away. "We're not out of the woods yet. I called for backup. I hear the sirens now. Let's get downstairs if we can."

She heard them, too. Sliding her shoulder beneath Nick's uninjured arm, she wrapped her arms around his waist and helped him walk toward the stairs.

"What about this guy?" he asked, pointing his gun toward the man on the lab floor.

"He's dead. I blew him up."

"Way to use that science, slugger." She felt the chuckle vibrate in his chest, then felt the flinch of pain. "Oh, damn."

"Nick, you need to sit down." She leaned him against the wall and helped him slide down to the floor. She slipped out of her lab coat and dropped to her knees beside him, wadding up the coat and pressing it against the wound in his shoulder.

He moaned and thanked her in the same breath.

"So The Cleaner's a woman. And for some sick reason, she's destroying any evidence that could lead us to identify our unsub?"

"In a nutshell."

Nick set his gun on the floor beside him and pulled his phone off his belt to punch in a number. "Maybe she wants to be the one to capture that bastard, not us. I need to fill in Spencer. Get the rest of the task force on this."

"Nick, enough playing detective." She pressed a little harder against his shoulder, cringing when he sucked in his breath. "Are your ribs hurt, too?"

He nodded as he let her take the phone from his unresisting fingers to set it beside the gun. "Just for the record, what color were Kapoor's eyes?"

"Brown. He's the man who attacked me in the alley."

"I knew I'd seen those eyes before."

"That's how The Cleaner and those reporters knew I'd been hurt. How she knew where I'd be. How to ensure I was the CSI at Brian Elliott's warehouse. Raj was an inside man, leaking information."

"Why the hell would he betray his own people? We're trying to save the city."

"I think Raj has a gambling problem. He owes somebody something he can't pay and she exploited that. She was probably holding something over both these men, blackmailing them into doing her dirty work."

"All four of them. Both the guards were fakes, too."

"Four?" She unfolded part of the lab coat and dabbed at the scratches along his jaw. Tears stung her eyes to think of all this man had done for her. "You really do have an overevolved protective instinct, don't you?"

"Guess so." He pushed aside the hands that were trying to doctor him and caught her by the nape of her neck, tunneling his fingers into her hair. He gripped her a little too tightly, his handsome face strained with the anguish he was feeling. "You're killing me, Annie Hermann."

"I'm sorry." She immediately pulled away, hurting herself to think she'd caused him more pain. "I didn't mean—"

He caught her again, pulling her onto his lap and threading his fingers into her hair to hold her close. "You're killing me because you keep trying to die and I don't want to lose you."

Annie framed his face between her hands and smiled, taking a risk she never thought she would again. "You won't lose me, Nick. Ever. I love you."

"I love you." Those killer blue eyes looked deep into her heart and claimed it. He pulled her to his chest and claimed her mouth, too, in a kiss that was hard and thorough and deep.

She wound her arms around his neck and leaned into his chest, opening her mouth to let his tongue slide against hers, opening her heart to let him understand everything she felt for him. There were moans of pain and sheer happiness and thanks and desire, and still they kissed.

They kissed until she heard footsteps on the stairs and Spencer Montgomery shouting their names.

With a reluctant gasp, Nick pulled his lips from hers. His fingers sifted through the curls of her hair, then stroked her face, her neck, her lips. "So where do we go from here? I'm never quite sure what to say or do around you. I don't want you to think about this too much and change your mind."

"I won't." She traced the same path across his face and hair. "How about we start with the one place where we've never had an argument?"

He crooked that handsome grin. "What's that?"

"Let's buy season tickets for the Royals."

Nick laughed out loud and Annie joined him. "Love to, slugger." He wound his uninjured arm around her and kissed her again. "I'd love to."

* * * * *

USA TODAY *bestselling author*
Julie Miller's heart-stopping miniseries
The Precinct: Task Force continues in
June 2013 with ASSUMED IDENTITY.
Look for it wherever
Harlequin Intrigue books are sold!

LARGER-PRINT BOOKS!
GET 2 FREE LARGER-PRINT NOVELS PLUS 2 FREE GIFTS!

HARLEQUIN®

INTRIGUE®

BREATHTAKING ROMANTIC SUSPENSE

YES! Please send me 2 FREE LARGER-PRINT Harlequin Intrigue® novels and my 2 FREE gifts (gifts are worth about $10). After receiving them, if I don't wish to receive any more books, I can return the shipping statement marked "cancel." If I don't cancel, I will receive 6 brand-new novels every month and be billed just $5.24 per book in the U.S. or $5.99 per book in Canada. That's a saving of at least 13% off the cover price! It's quite a bargain! Shipping and handling is just 50¢ per book in the U.S. and 75¢ per book in Canada.* I understand that accepting the 2 free books and gifts places me under no obligation to buy anything. I can always return a shipment and cancel at any time. Even if I never buy another book, the two free books and gifts are mine to keep forever.

199/399 HDN FVQ7

Name	(PLEASE PRINT)

Address	Apt. #

City	State/Prov.	Zip/Postal Code

Signature (if under 18, a parent or guardian must sign)

Mail to the Harlequin® Reader Service:
IN U.S.A.: P.O. Box 1867, Buffalo, NY 14240-1867
IN CANADA: P.O. Box 609, Fort Erie, Ontario L2A 5X3

**Are you a subscriber to Harlequin Intrigue books
and want to receive the larger-print edition?
Call 1-800-873-8635 today or visit www.ReaderService.com.**

* Terms and prices subject to change without notice. Prices do not include applicable taxes. Sales tax applicable in N.Y. Canadian residents will be charged applicable taxes. Offer not valid in Quebec. This offer is limited to one order per household. Not valid for current subscribers to Harlequin Intrigue Larger-Print books. All orders subject to credit approval. Credit or debit balances in a customer's account(s) may be offset by any other outstanding balance owed by or to the customer. Please allow 4 to 6 weeks for delivery. Offer available while quantities last.

Your Privacy—The Harlequin® Reader Service is committed to protecting your privacy. Our Privacy Policy is available online at www.ReaderService.com or upon request from the Harlequin Reader Service.

We make a portion of our mailing list available to reputable third parties that offer products we believe may interest you. If you prefer that we not exchange your name with third parties, or if you wish to clarify or modify your communication preferences, please visit us at www.ReaderService.com/consumerchoice or write to us at Harlequin Reader Service Preference Service, P.O. Box 9062, Buffalo, NY 14269. Include your complete name and address.

HILP13

ReaderService.com

Manage your account online!

- Review your order history
- Manage your payments
- Update your address

*We've designed
the Harlequin® Reader Service
website just for you.*

Enjoy all the features!

- Reader excerpts from any series
- Respond to mailings and
  special monthly offers
- Discover new series available to you
- Browse the Bonus Bucks catalog
- Share your feedback

Visit us at:
ReaderService.com

RS13

REQUEST YOUR FREE BOOKS!

2 FREE NOVELS
PLUS 2 FREE GIFTS!

WORLDWIDE LIBRARY®
Your Partner in Crime

YES! Please send me 2 FREE novels from the Worldwide Library® series and my 2 FREE gifts (gifts are worth about $10). After receiving them, if I don't wish to receive any more books, I can return the shipping statement marked "cancel." If I don't cancel, I will receive 4 brand-new novels every month and be billed just $5.24 per book in the U.S. or $6.24 per book in Canada. That's a savings of at least 34% off the cover price. It's quite a bargain! Shipping and handling is just 50¢ per book in the U.S. and 75¢ per book in Canada.* I understand that accepting the 2 free books and gifts places me under no obligation to buy anything. I can always return a shipment and cancel at any time. Even if I never buy another book, the two free books and gifts are mine to keep forever.

414/424 WDN FVUV

Name	(PLEASE PRINT)

Address	Apt. #

City	State/Prov.	Zip/Postal Code

Signature (if under 18, a parent or guardian must sign)

Mail to the **Harlequin® Reader Service:**
IN U.S.A.: P.O. Box 1867, Buffalo, NY 14240-1867
IN CANADA: P.O. Box 609, Fort Erie, Ontario L2A 5X3

Want to try two free books from another line?
Call 1-800-873-8635 or visit www.ReaderService.com.

* Terms and prices subject to change without notice. Prices do not include applicable taxes. Sales tax applicable in N.Y. Canadian residents will be charged applicable taxes. Offer not valid in Quebec. This offer is limited to one order per household. Not valid for current subscribers to the Worldwide Library series. All orders subject to credit approval. Credit or debit balances in a customer's account(s) may be offset by any other outstanding balance owed by or to the customer. Please allow 4 to 6 weeks for delivery. Offer available while quantities last.

Your Privacy—The Harlequin® Reader Service is committed to protecting your privacy. Our Privacy Policy is available online at www.ReaderService.com or upon request from the Harlequin Reader Service.

We make a portion of our mailing list available to reputable third parties that offer products we believe may interest you. If you prefer that we not exchange your name with third parties, or if you wish to clarify or modify your communication preferences, please visit us at www.ReaderService.com/consumerschoice or write to us at Harlequin Reader Service Preference Service, P.O. Box 9062, Buffalo, NY 14269. Include your complete name and address.

WWLI3